"What exactly are you offering me?" Cristiano asked, finding his gaze intent on Julienne's. He did nothing to temper it. **"And more important, why are you offering it?"**

"You could have taken what I was offering ten years ago. You didn't."

He gazed down at the hand she'd laid on his arm as if it was a writhing, poisonous snake. When he raised his gaze to hers once more, he felt certain it was frigid.

Yet somehow, she did not retreat.

"Are you suggesting that because I did not behave like an animal then, I might reverse course now?" He blinked in an astonishment that was in no way exaggerated. "I don't know what is more offensive. That you think I require pity sex or, worse, that you imagine I might accept it."

He had meant to sound cold. Exacting. And yet somehow the word *sex* seemed to linger between them, making its own weather.

"That's not what I meant to suggest at all."

Passion in Paradise

Exotic escapes...and red-hot romances!

Step into a jet-set world where first class is the *only* way to travel. From Monte Carlo to Tuscany, you'll find a billionaire at every turn! But no billionaire is complete without the perfect romance. Especially when that passion is found in the most incredible destinations...

Find out what happens in:

The Innocent's Forgotten Wedding by Lynne Graham

The Italian's Pregnant Cinderella by Caitlin Crews

Kidnapped for His Royal Heir by Maya Blake

His Greek Wedding Night Debt by Michelle Smart

The Spaniard's Surprise Love-Child by Kim Lawrence

My Shocking Monte Carlo Confession by Heidi Rice

A Bride Fit for a Prince? by Susan Stephens

A Scandal Made in London by Lucy King

Available this month!

Caitlin Crews

—

THE ITALIAN'S PREGNANT CINDERELLA

HHARLEQUIN

PRESENTS

HARLEQUIN®
PRESENTS®

Recycling programs
for this product may
not exist in your area.

ISBN-13: 978-1-335-14842-1

The Italian's Pregnant Cinderella

Copyright © 2020 by Caitlin Crews

This edition published by arrangement with Harlequin Books S.A.

For questions and comments about the quality of this book,
please contact us at CustomerService@Harlequin.com.

Harlequin Enterprises ULC
22 Adelaide St. West, 40th Floor
Toronto, Ontario M5H 4E3, Canada
www.Harlequin.com

Printed in U.S.A.

USA TODAY bestselling and RITA® Award–nominated author **Caitlin Crews** loves writing romance. She teaches her favorite romance novels in creative-writing classes at places like UCLA Extension's prestigious Writers' Program, where she finally gets to utilize the MA and PhD in English literature she received from the University of York in England. She currently lives in the Pacific Northwest with her very own hero and too many pets. Visit her at caitlincrews.com.

CHAPTER ONE

MONACO AGAIN.

It was fitting, really.

Julienne Boucher had been working toward this moment with single-minded passion and bone-deep determination for the past ten years, and it made a certain sense that when she crossed the finish line at long last, she would do it here. At the Grand Hotel in Monte Carlo where she had first come ten years ago.

To sell herself.

Julienne's perilously high heels clicked against the sumptuous marble floors of the Grand Hotel as she walked, passing the flower arrangements that had looked like colorful, exotic jungles to her unsophisticated eyes back then. The lobby had been just as smugly opulent, but the difference was that back then, she'd been terrified that everyone was looking at her. That they knew what she'd come to do. That they could *see* her shame and panic, and more, her determination to go ahead and do it anyway.

Because she had to.

She'd wondered if the horrible men in the village she'd come from—and had escaped earlier that same day—had been right all along. That Boucher women were made for one thing only, the whores. And if that was true, could *everyone* see that truth all over her? Or was it more of a bad smell…in this place that was lightly scented with ease and wealth and refinement?

Now she knew that if anyone bothered to look at her, what they would see was the elegant, self-possessed woman she'd fought so hard to become. Day by day. Year by year. A woman who was not only sophisticated, but looked as if she belonged in hotels like this one that were more properly works of art.

Because she did. She'd made sure she did.

Julienne could almost see the ghost of her former self walking beside her, reflecting all those nerves and that bone-deep desolation back from the gilt-edged, shiny surfaces, the fragrant orchids, the giddy chandeliers.

This time around, she was healthy. Well fed and well clothed instead of balancing on the precarious edge of total destruction, homeless and penniless. Most important, she was no longer a desperate teenager. No longer a scared sixteen-year-old, bleakly determined to do what she had to do to save her younger sister. Even if that meant losing herself.

Thinking of Fleurette cut through the haunting memories of ten years back and Julienne paused, there outside the famously luxurious lounge bar that catered to the world's wealthiest. Something she had guessed at then, but knew for a fact now.

Fleurette did not believe in ghosts. She had grown these last ten years, too, and was no longer a fragile waif, sickly and scared. These days Julienne's younger sister was a force to be reckoned with in every regard. From her brash sleeves of brightly colored tattoos to her defiant piercings and multicolored hair forever cut short, Fleurette made it clear with her every word and deed that she would never be *desperate* again. For anything.

"You've finally done it," Fleurette had said with her usual brisk impatience when Julienne had called her earlier. "That last deal has to be worth billions alone. I think we can both agree that you've adequately repaid the man's kindness. In spades."

Julienne had made an assenting noise, but she wasn't as certain as her sister. About anything, if she was honest—but particularly about this.

Because Cristiano Cassara had saved them. And not in a metaphoric sense. He had literally saved their lives that evening ten years ago when he could as easily have hastened their decline or simply ignored their predicament altogether. He had kept the two of them from a dark spiral into almost certain death on the streets—if not that night, then not long after it, because that was how that particular trajectory went. Julienne knew that all too well. But she hadn't had to test herself against a downward slope into hell that ate girls just like her alive every day. Because Cristiano had whisked both Julienne and Fleurette away into a brand-new life, asked for nothing in return and had left them to it with no interference.

Which meant that repaying him for what he'd done had consumed Julienne's life ever since.

She had followed him here, to the place it was rumored he came to relax once a year—though Julienne could not imagine the stern, austere head of the Cassara Corporation allowing his spine to curve the faintest inch, much less *relaxing* in any meaningful way. Julienne had worked for the man for almost ten full years and had never seen the faintest stirrings of a smile on his forbidding face.

Not even a *hint*.

Julienne blew out a long breath and checked her appearance for the hundredth time in one of the shiny mirrors that graced nearly every wall and surface, the better to reflect back to the rich and famous their most favorite view of all—themselves.

Another thing it had taken years to learn. No

one in a place like this had time to look at others. Not when they were so busy gazing at themselves.

The truth was, she already knew full well that she was groomed to perfection.

That had been part of the payment she had offered her benefactor from almost the first, though he had never asked for such a thing. Nor noticed that she'd provided it.

But then, she was the one who had been there that night ten years ago, right here in this hotel. She was the one who'd taken her sister and run from the vicious little hill town where they'd been born, abandoned and repeatedly betrayed by what little family they'd had, supposed friends, and vindictive neighbors. All of whom had known what kind of women they were going to become since birth, and had always, always treated them accordingly.

Julienne had used her last handful of euros to buy the bus tickets to get the two of them out of the dead-end place, choked on the fumes of feuds ages old. She'd brazenly stolen a dress from a rack outside a boutique in the Centre Commercial de Fontvieille.

And then, she'd snuck into a bathroom, and done herself up the best she could. The pretty dress. The cheap heels. The lipstick she'd saved from their long-dead mother, though it was crumbling and sad after so long. Enough eye makeup to disguise her shame.

And hopefully her fear, too, which she'd been afraid might have a scent all its own. Acrid. Sharp. Obvious.

She'd snuck into the Grand Hotel, leaving Fleurette hidden as best she could in an alley. Terrified that she'd be grabbed and tossed out at any moment, she'd found her way to the very bar she was approaching now. Back then she'd been astonished by the place, particularly the deep, shining wood that ached with pedigrees and fat purses. Better still, it had been filled with her quarry.

Rich men.

Who everyone knew were more than happy to purchase anything.

Including sixteen-year-old girls desperate for some cash.

Julienne had learned that lesson back in the village, where she had declined the butcher's offer to toss her a few coins if she "made him happy." It wasn't his bad teeth or that he smelled like blood, though neither had helped. It was that she'd already known what became of girls like her who listened to the promises of older men in that town. Or any men in that town. She was the result of her own mother's bad decisions years back, and she knew where they ended. Strung out and eventually dead, leaving behind two daughters to the same fate.

If it was her fate, Julienne had decided, she would face it. But not in that place of echoes, built vertically into a cold hillside and filled with all the people who had watched her mother spiral into horror without lifting a finger to help. She would take Fleurette and go south to glittering Monaco, where at least their own inevitable spiral would gleam a good deal brighter all the way down.

Tonight Julienne bore no resemblance to that gaunt, terrified child. Her hair was a fall of fine caramel, polished to shine, and she wore it twisted back into a deceptively effortless chignon. She was not wearing a stolen dress—the balance for which she'd left, years later, at that same boutique with a note of apology. Julienne had built herself into a sophisticated professional in these intervening years. She preferred sleek pencil skirts and the feeling of real silk against her skin, no less than what was expected for a woman with a big job at a multinational company. She favored statement heels and understated pearls at her ears, complete with a slim gold watch on her wrist.

Cristiano Cassara had done that, too. He'd given her the means not only to become the best version of herself possible, but to repay her debts. And to change her world.

Now it was time to change it again.

Julienne paused a few steps into the lush, dimly lit bar. She looked around, seeing what could have been the same old men, rich and jaded, lounging at the same tables. Then she looked toward the expanse of the bar itself, and it was as if he'd planned it.

As if he remembered, too.

Because Cristiano Cassara sat where she remembered him, there at a bar so glossy and luxurious that sixteen-year-old Julienne had gaped at it as if all those bottles lined up so prettily were precious jewels.

This time, her heart beat hard against her ribs again, but it wasn't fear.

It was a heady mix of victory and regret, and a strong dose of anticipation, for good measure.

She headed toward him, ready to do this at last.

Cristiano Cassara had been beautiful enough ten years ago, for all he had seemed remote. Carved from the same stone as the statues that graced the wide hall that had led her here. He'd been a relatively young man then, yet already wealthier than Julienne could have possibly imagined. The heir apparent to the Cassara chocolate fortune, he had worn his wealth and consequence in the cut of the exquisite suit he'd worn and in the very breadth of his shoulders. Not to mention the way he regarded the world around him, as if it, too, belonged to him.

Not that Julienne had known any of that, then. She'd looked at him and known that he was wealthy, that was all.

Tonight, he was all of that and more, a study in sheer masculine power.

She took a moment to really gaze at him, because this was not a Cassara Corporation boardroom where she'd always had too much to prove to waste her time making eyes at a man who she was fairly certain saw only numbers, profits and losses in return. In all the meetings she'd ever attended with him, Cristiano was steely, edging toward grim. He made no attempt to disguise his ruthlessness, and dispensed praise so sparingly that Julienne rather thought an actual murmur of vague approval might send her into a swoon.

Something that had never been put to the test.

Cristiano had been wealthy ten years ago. Today he was one of the richest men alive. She knew that if she looked around, she would likely find his security detail fanned out around the bar, unobtrusively keeping tabs on the man whose annual net worth was a number so vast that most people were unable to fully grasp it. There were too many zeroes. She would no doubt also see the hungry eyes of the women who trailed after him wherever he went, singed through but never quite burned to ash by all his steel and banked flame. She might even see the sneers of men who imagined him their rival, when it was obvious he was without peer.

As far as Julienne was concerned, he was perfect.

Sixteen-year-old Julienne had made a beeline

for him because he was closest. And because, after her first, terrified look around this bar for a likely first client, he had been the only one in the place without gray hair. A fat belly. Or both.

She had told herself then that if she must do the thing, far better to do it with a man like him, who songs could have been written about. And likely had been.

She'd walked up to him, desperation making her bold enough to put a hand on his arm. And she had waited for him to look away from the drink that sat before him on the bar, seemingly untouched.

When he'd raised his gaze to hers, it had burned.

He was too intense, they said. Too harsh. Needlessly grim and cold for a man who made sweets.

But Julienne thought he had a poet's mouth, for all that it was forever in that same flat line. His dark hair was thick and had yet to surrender to the ravages of age. It wasn't only that he kept himself in such magnificent shape, though that helped add to his mystique. It was that he seemed far larger and more threatening than he was. A vast giant lurking in the form of a man. As if the shadow he cast could engulf anyone unwary enough to venture close.

But by the time Julienne had realized that ten years ago, it had been too late.

Her hand had been on his arm.

Her heart had nearly exploded from her chest.

"Would you like to buy me a drink?" Julienne had asked the man with the eyes that burned, her voice squeaking with panic.

That was what a girl said, she'd been told by brittle, hard edged Annette, who had never been much of a mother. Every time Annette went off to what she called her *parties*, she came back with less of herself. As if someone had reached inside her, scraped out everything in there and left her to walk around an empty hollow.

She had died when Julienne was fourteen and everyone had called it a blessing.

Julienne had intended to survive, no matter how hollow she was inside. And unlike Annette, Julienne did not plan to forget her obligations to Fleurette, who had only been ten, then. She would take care of her sister if it killed her. And she would not consign Fleurette to the same fate.

At least one of them should survive without that scraped-out emptiness. Just one.

"How old are you?" he had replied, in richly compelling French blurred slightly with an Italian accent. Julienne hadn't expected the question. Who knew men were discerning—about anything? Her experience so far had not allowed for the possibility. She drew in a breath, prepared to claim she was a more palatable eighteen, despite the fact sixteen was perfectly legal. But his dark eyes flashed as if he knew what she meant to do. "Don't lie to me."

"Old enough," she replied, trying to sound husky. Throaty. Wasn't that how women sounded in situations like this? "Past the age of consent, if that is what you mean."

He had looked at her, through her. In her whole life, before and since, Julienne had never felt so *seen*. In that moment she was certain that Cristiano Cassara could see everything. *Everything*. What had happened, what she'd had planned. The one-way spiral of the life before her and the squalid bleakness she'd left behind. Fleurette out there in an alley, the emptiness in Julienne's wallet and belly alike, and what she was prepared to do to change both.

All the things she was prepared to do, starting here. With him.

More than that, she was certain he could also see the dreams and hopes she had long since jettisoned in her committed attempts to keep her sister and her warm and reasonably fed—if never safe or happy.

"I rather think not," he had said, a quiet thunder stroke of a comment.

And then Cristiano Cassara had changed her life.

With a lift of one hand.

The déjà vu was intense tonight. Cristiano again sat at the bar, another untouched drink before him.

He fiddled with it, turning it this way and that, but he did not lift it to his lips. She now knew the rumors about him—every rumor, in fact. That he never drank, that his father had loved his liquor too well but his wife and child too little, and that these were the rituals Cristiano performed when he was alone. The untouched drink. The sober vigil.

He still had that poet's mouth, with its hint of sensuality she had never seen him succumb to, not once. Not even in the odd, stolen paparazzi shot of him when he couldn't have known he was being watched. His face was a terrible kind of beautiful, harsh and brutal, with cheekbones that made a woman dream of saints and martyrs. And those dark, flashing eyes that still burned when he looked at a person directly.

She remembered what his arm had felt like beneath her hand as if her palm was a scar. All that hard, hot power.

And Julienne was not a child any longer. She was not a scared teenager, prepared to sell herself to the highest bidder—or any bidder at all—because she was devoid of options and out of choices.

Still, there was a particular agony to this moment, so long in coming.

She slid her bejeweled evening purse onto the glossy bar, and angled her body toward his.

And knew, without his having glanced her way or indicated he was anything but alone, that he had been aware of her all along. Perhaps even before she'd stepped inside the dark, deliberately close space.

But she was too good at making him into a myth, as Fleurette often complained. Tonight she planned to focus on the man.

Cristiano had succeeded his grandfather to become the CEO and president of the company not long after she'd met him ten years ago. More than that, and more importantly, he was Julienne's boss. She had started at the company headquarters in Milan ten years ago, as a part-time job she fit in around the private studies Cristiano had arranged for her and Fleurette. First she'd been an intern. And then, once she'd finished her schooling at eighteen, she'd taken the lowest position offered and had worked her way steadily up.

That she was, in effect, Cristiano's ward had never signified. It was never discussed, and Julienne often wondered if anyone else even knew how generous he was, or how she had personally benefitted from it. But then, it wasn't as if she'd ever lived with him. He had put them up in one of his houses in Milan, complete with staff to tend to them, and in essence, they'd raised themselves.

We were too old already, Fleurette liked to say.

These days, Julienne lived across the sea in New York City. She'd fought hard to get to her position as the vice president of North American operations for the Cassara Corporation, reporting directly to

Cristiano himself. And she'd fought even harder to close the kind of deals that would not only pay Cristiano back for his generosity all those years ago, but give back more than he'd given.

It had taken years.

He looked at her now, that dark gaze of his cool and assessing.

But no less harsh.

She would have felt let down if it had been, she understood.

"Thank you for coming," she said, as politely as if she was looking at him across a table in one of the Cassara Corporation's many offices.

"You were insistent, Ms. Boucher," he said, and there was that undercurrent of disapproval in his voice that let her know that he was astonished that she'd dared. And that she'd persisted, despite his secretary's best efforts.

Julienne smiled, still polite and calm. "You met me here once before."

And she knew as she said it that she was breaking all their rules. The unspoken boundaries all three of them had maintained for a decade. She and Fleurette never mentioned him or how they'd made it from a sad, half-abandoned French hill town to a lavishly appointed, semidetached townhouse in the center of Milan. He never indicated he knew either one of them. Sometimes Julienne had worried that he'd forgotten what he'd done for them—that it had meant so little to him when it had altered the whole of hers and Fleurette's lives.

But no, she could see he hadn't forgotten. More, she could see his astonishment, there in his eyes like a thread of gold in the brown depths. His dark brows rose, and he looked almost...arrested.

"I did." His study of her made her want to shake. She didn't, somehow. Not outwardly. "A meeting neither one of us has referenced in a decade. To what do I owe the pleasure of this unexpected trip down memory lane, Ms. Boucher?"

His voice was crisp. A distinct and deliberate slap, though as stern and controlled as everything else he did.

He meant her to wilt and she wanted to, but then, she had built herself in his image. She was made of sterner stuff because he was, and because she'd always assumed he expected it. She kept her cool smile on her face.

"In that decade, I have kept track of what you must have spent to rescue Fleurette and me. Then care for us." She named a staggering number and saw that light in his eyes change again, to something far more sharp and assessing that she could feel like a fist in her belly. And lower, like heat. "With the latest deal we closed and the amount I have in a separate fund with your name on it, I believe I have repaid that sum. With interest."

His eyes were dark brown, like the bittersweet

chocolate his family made. And yet that could hardly begin to describe their ferocity, or the intense way they narrowed on her now.

"I do not recall asking for repayment. Or even acknowledgment."

"Nonetheless." She took a deep breath. "My resignation letter waits for you in Milan."

He blinked. "I beg your pardon. You are resigning?"

"I am. I have."

She reached out and did what she'd done ten years ago. She put her hand on his arm, but this time, she meant it.

Oh, how she meant it.

"Cristiano," she said quietly. Invitingly, she hoped. "Would you like to buy me that drink?"

CHAPTER TWO

CRISTIANO CASSARA DID NOT care for surprises.

He had arranged his life with great precision, the better to avoid the unpleasant shock of events that went in directions he had not already foreseen. Cristiano had a deep and abiding dismay for chaos or mess of any kind, thanks to a childhood brimming over with nothing but, and had therefore dedicated himself to organizing as much of the world as possible to suit his requirements.

Something that was easier than perhaps it ought to have been when one was a Cassara.

He should have deeply disliked the fact that this woman had deliberately shifted the ground beneath their feet. That she had not stayed put in the compartment where he'd placed her years ago.

He told himself he did.

But it was too late. Something in him had shifted, too, without a care for how little he liked the sensation. And he suddenly found himself looking at Julienne Boucher as if he'd never seen her before.

As if she was a beautiful woman he'd happened to meet in a bar in Monte Carlo, instead of all the other things she'd been to him over time. His attempt at kindness, at a kind of redemption. The embodiment of his guilt. And possibly the best vice president the Cassara Corporation had ever had, save himself.

"What exactly are you offering me?" he asked, finding his gaze intent on hers. He did nothing to temper it. "And more important, why are you offering it?"

"You could have taken what I was offering ten years ago. You didn't."

He gazed down at the hand she'd laid on his arm as if it was a writhing, poisonous snake. When he raised his gaze to hers once more, he felt certain it was frigid.

Yet somehow, she did not retreat.

"Are you suggesting that because I did not behave like an animal then I might reverse course now?" He blinked in an astonishment that was in no way exaggerated. "I don't know what is more offensive. That you think I require pity sex or worse, that you imagine I might accept it."

He had meant to sound cold. Exacting. And yet somehow the word *sex* seemed to linger between them, making its own weather.

"That's not what I meant to suggest at all."

And through the kick of the temper he usually fought much harder to keep under wraps, he was aware that Julienne did not seem upset. She gazed back at him calmly, her face open and her eyes clear, and he was forced to think back to all the other times this woman had sat before him in her other role. As his employee.

Which was the only way he had thought about her since she'd joined the company as an intern approximately a thousand years ago. He had watched her meteoric rise from intern to vice president with a detached sort of interest, the way he would have noted any other rapid ascent, and he had sat in many meetings face-to-face with her coolness. Cristiano would not have had said he'd admired the way she handled herself, but he had appreciated it. On behalf of the Cassara Corporation, of course.

It occurred to him now that she was not afraid of him. Not intimidated in the least, which was unusual.

Remarkable, even.

"I have always been enormously grateful to you," she said, leaving her viper of a hand where it was. Cristiano had the notion he could feel the heat of it through the fine wool of the suit his tailors had crafted precisely for the late October weather, when that was unlikely. As unlikely as the wholly unexpected response his body was having to her. "How could I not be? And I always planned to repay you, because that is the decent thing to do, is it not?"

His mouth was full of ice, it seemed. "It is unnecessary."

"To you, yes. Which only makes it more necessary to me."

Again he stared down at her hand, trying to recall the last time someone had dared place a hand upon him without an invitation and his express permission. Nothing came to mind.

Not even his father had dared, after a certain point. When Cristiano had finally grown too tall.

And the longer her hand rested there on his forearm, the less unpleasant he found it, no matter what he told himself. Quite the opposite, in fact. That heat instead seemed to wind through him, a peculiar treachery.

There were more betrayals. The longer she stood there, too close to him, he *noticed* things. He noticed *her*. Her narrow, elegant fingers. The carefully polished nails, in a quietly sophisticated shade that made him think of what her skin might look like, flushed with pleasure against smooth sheets.

Unbidden, Cristiano remembered the last time she'd put her hand on him, here in this same bar a lifetime ago. He couldn't say he'd thought about it since—and yet now he suddenly had a perfect recollection of her same hand in the same place, though she had been altogether rougher then. Her nails had been ragged and untended, or bitten down to the quick. And her eyes had been glazed with misery and fear, not…

But he did not wish to define what it was he saw in Julienne's gaze just then.

No matter his body's enthusiastic response.

"The Cassara Corporation has been mother and father to me," Julienne said, with a soft intensity that he ordered himself to ignore. But couldn't. "A family as well as a job. But you were the one who saved me. Right here. And then again and again over the years by providing me every opportunity to save myself. So I did, but all the while, I had you there as a guide. Or a goal, maybe."

"If you mean in a business sense, I must tell you, Ms. Boucher, that this is no way to go about—"

Her hand tightened on his arm. Cristiano felt the sensation race through him like an electric shock.

"It's not about business. Or why would I resign?" Julienne looked far more composed than he felt, and Cristiano hardly knew how to account for such a thing. "I wanted to repay our debt to you in ten years. I've done that now. But as those ten years passed, I found myself wishing that I could convince you to take my initial offer, after all."

When he glared at her, she only smiled. "Not for money, of course. I'm not in the same circumstances I was then. I'm not sixteen. I'm an adult woman, no longer your employee, and fully in control of her own faculties. I am not coerced. I am not desperate. When I found out you were going to be in Monaco again so soon after my last deal went through, it seemed the perfect bookend."

"A 'bookend'?" Cristiano repeated, and it was bad enough that he was looking at her now. Truly *seeing* her, after so long making it his business to act as if she wasn't quite there.

It was distinctly uncomfortable.

Because Julienne might have been a scraggly, terrified teenager ten years ago, covered in too much mascara and obvious misery. But that version of her was gone. She had grown into a beautiful woman, whether he chose to admit it or not. Her hair gleamed that burnished gold and brown that made him…hungry. Her eyes were too clever by half, fixed on him with an intensity and a sincerity that made his blood heat.

And he would have to be a dead man not to notice that her body, no longer packaged in a tacky dress that had been much too old for her, was a quiet symphony of curves and grace.

Cristiano did not indulge himself with his employees, as a matter of honor and good business sense alike. Both virtues, to his mind, and both traits his own father had distinctly lacked.

But Julienne had tendered her resignation.

And enveloped as they were in the dim embrace of a quiet bar tucked away in the midst of Monte Carlo's frenetic opulence, he could hardly remember why he should have objected to any of this in the first place.

Julienne did not know it, but she was already connected to him in ways that would have made him far more than merely *uncomfortable*, had he allowed the strict compartments he kept inside him to open wide at any point in the past ten years. He never had.

He wasn't sure he wanted to now, but her hand was on his arm and there was that *heat*—

Cristiano had not been in this specific bar by chance ten years ago. He disliked Monaco intensely, associating it as he did with the worst of his father's notorious excesses. It had been in this very bar that he had indulged in the last of those terrible scenes with Giacomo Cassara. His father had been cruel. Cristiano had returned the favor. And he had been sitting right here, staring at his father's favorite drink—the demon Giacomo had carried about on his back, night and day, for as long as Cristiano could remember, wondering at his own descent into cruelty and what it might herald—when Julienne had appeared beside him.

He had been engaged in nothing less than a battle for his own soul that night. The endless war with his father was one of attrition, and any victories Cristiano scored grew more Pyrrhic by the day. He had begun to wonder if it was worth attempting to live up to his grandfather's antiquated notions of honor when Giacomo was so busy dedicating himself to living down to every expectation.

Cristiano had been raised by two men, one a saint and one a devil, and that night he'd been wavering between them.

That was the mess that Julienne Boucher had walked in on, tottering on heels she clearly didn't yet know how to walk in.

He had glanced up to find her there beside him, as pale as she was determined. And there had never been any question that he might help himself to her, as his tastes ran to the enthusiastic, not the unwilling. Or the transactional. He'd felt for a moment as if he had his grandfather on one shoulder and his father on the other.

And in the middle stood a girl with poverty all over her like the too-tight dress she wore and a fixed smile on her too-young face, offering herself to him.

Cristiano had not been tempted to sample her wares. He wasn't remotely interested in teenagers, heaven forbid. And he certainly did not troll for sex from the streets. But it had taken him a beat too long to say so. To brush off the whispering devil spilling poison into his ear—the one telling him to ignore her, the one insisting she wasn't his problem when he had enough of his own, the one who wanted him to turn his back on her and get back to his already messy evening—and do what was right.

That he had wavered at all, that he was that selfish, disgusted him.

And perhaps that was why he had not simply given her some money from his pocket and gone on his way. It was the guilt he couldn't shake that had made him go further. It was the stain of his shame that had turned him into her benefactor.

To prove that he was nothing like his father.

Even if, later that same night, he had learned that in truth, he was worse.

But tonight, Julienne did not come to him as a desperate child determined to sell her body for survival. She came to him as a woman, and a beautiful one at that, with a body she could have shared with any man in Monaco, if she so chose.

And still she'd chosen him.

He couldn't deny he liked the symmetry of it.

Cristiano couldn't go back in time and change that brief, terrible moment when he'd very nearly turned his back on the girl she'd been. Very nearly abandoning her to her fate with whatever jackals populated places like this. Vile men like his own father, selfish and destructive and heedless of the damage he caused.

So easily could Cristiano have broken her and

condemned her younger sister, too, simply by walking away from Julienne that night.

He carried the weight of that, two bright lives he could have extinguished in one fell swoop, around with him. They were an enduring reminder of how close he'd come to becoming more like his father, the cost of housing and educating and outfitting them negligible to a man of his wealth—and a small dent indeed next to the soul he'd nearly lost.

They had been an act of kindness to prove he had it in him. Then an act of penance for the other things he'd lost that night.

One way or another, Julienne and her sister had long been his personal cross to bear.

And it was tempting, oh, so tempting, to put them down once and for all.

"Are you going to answer me?" Julienne asked, and she tilted her head slightly to one side as she asked it, once again signaling how little she was intimidated by him. It was a novel experience. Cristiano should have been outraged at her temerity. Her lack of respect.

Instead, he found himself intrigued.

"How can I?" he replied after a moment. "I don't know what it is you are offering."

"Me. I'm offering me."

"I appreciate the offer. And that you are no longer making it while barely legal." He considered her, the light from behind the bar making her face seem very nearly luminous. "But you see, I have rules."

"I've worked for you for ten years, Mr. Cassara. If, all of a sudden, you did not have rules for every given situation, *that* would be concerning."

He thought of his guilt, his shame. That brief, glaring moment when he had understood himself to be no better than the father he disdained with every particle of his being. The father who had humiliated him, rampaged through his childhood and laughed in the face of his pain.

How easy would it be to wash that moment away. He had saved the girl, after all. And the result of what he'd actually done—instead of merely *thought*—was Julienne.

Julienne, the youngest vice president in the history of the Cassara Corporation—aside from Cristiano himself.

Julienne, who looked at him without the calculation he had grown to expect in the eyes of women who dared attempt to get close to him— or rather, to his plump bank accounts. Julienne, whose toffee-colored eyes were filled with heat. Longing, even.

He had come back to this terrible place at least once each year since that night to stand a vigil. To remember who he'd nearly become.

Maybe, a voice in him suggested, *it is time to let it go.*

Cristiano followed an urge he would normally have tamped down, hard, and reached across the scant inches between them. He fit his hand to the curve of her cheek, and traced his way down the delicate line of her neck to find the hollow of her throat. Then, lower, to the soft skin visible in the open neck of her silk blouse that hinted at her breasts below.

And watched in a dark delight as she flushed, bright and hot.

The precise shade of her nail polish.

"I do not do entanglements," he told her severely. Though he was questioning himself already, as the heat in her skin shot through him, pooling in his sex. His body was tight, ready. And suddenly, it was as if he'd spent years wanting nothing more than to drive himself deep and hard inside her. "I like sex, Ms. Boucher. But I do not traffic in emotional displays."

Her breath was choppy and her eyes were hot, but her voice was cool when she spoke. "I hope I have never given you reason to imagine that I was particularly emotional."

"The boardroom is not the bedroom."

"Indeed it is not. Or you would have found me distinctly indecent, long before now."

He liked the notion of that. And suddenly there were too many images in his head of missed opportunities in the office…the kinds of images he never allowed to pollute his mind. The kinds of images he kept behind the walls of all those compartments inside him, because to lose those separations was to become too much like his father. When he wanted instead to be like his grandfather, the man who had taught him how to build partitions. And use them.

But walls were coming down all around them tonight.

"You have always struck me as a woman who likes to be in charge." He continued to trace an absent pattern this way and that, in and around her low collar, drawing in the wild heat she generated. And far too aware of each breath she took. "But I'm afraid I am far too demanding for that."

Julienne shivered, as if the prospect of his demands was too delicious to bear, and he thought he might actually eat her alive. Here and now. Hoist her up on the bar and indulge himself at last.

That would be a bookend, indeed.

"What sort of demands do you mean?" she asked, and her voice changed. Gone was all that coolness, lost in a husky sort of heat that he could feel like a caress, there where he hungered for her the most.

It made him think of dark rooms, deep sighs.

He shifted again, and looked around, trying his best not to surrender to that drumming thing inside him. His blood, his pulse.

His need and his hunger.

Not cut out of him, as he'd believed all this time. But waiting.

Only waiting for a woman who dared.

But despite the riot inside him and the delicious idea he'd had concerning the bar, this was not the place to indulge himself. There were too many unfriendly eyes that watched his every move, especially in the moneyed halls of Monte Carlo, where too many well-fed enemies would leap at the chance to see and exploit his weaknesses.

Or his wants.

To Cristiano's mind, they were the same.

He took Julienne's hand in his and then he tugged her behind him, leading her back out of the dimly lit bar and into the hotel proper. He didn't look back at her. He didn't need to. He could see her in the mirrors they passed, looking flushed and ready.

He felt the pulse of greed deep in his sex.

Instead of leading her out into the grand lobby that was filled with guests and tourists alike, he moved deeper into the hotel. Then branched off into one of the smaller marble halls festooned with luxury shops. He kept going until he found an alcove, tucked between a shop filled with disgracefully overpriced perfume and another stocked entirely with nonsensical shoes.

And once there, away from prying eyes if not

entirely private, he backed her to the wall. Then propped himself over her there, one hand on either side of her head.

Cristiano watched, rapt, as she fought for breath.

How had he failed to truly *see* her all this time?

"Any and all demands," he said, finally answering her question. What demands, indeed. He could write a book or two and it would only skim the surface of the things he wanted. Needed. And would demand of her. "I like things the way I like them. Is that a problem for you?"

"I've been taking your orders for ten years."

He liked the way her eyes flashed. He liked that simmering defiance, right there beneath her cool exterior. He wanted to lick up all that elegance and see how she burned.

"One night, Julienne."

"You say that as if you imagine I might have started making a hope chest." She tossed her head with that same defiance and a streak of temper, too. "I assure you, Mr. Cassara, this is a sexual invitation. That's all."

"One night," he said again.

"I heard you the first time."

"It bears repeating, *cara*. I would hate for there to be any…confusion."

And he watched as another streak of temper made her toffee-colored eyes darken.

"How patronizing." And she scowled at him as

if he wasn't caging her against the wall. "I'm the one who propositioned you, in case you're the one who's confused. Twice, now. Perhaps that's what bears repeating."

"The only word I wish you to repeat is my name," he told her, low and dark, and leaned in then to get the scent of her in his nose. Sweet and hot at once. His pulse thickened, beating hard into his sex. "No more of this *Mr. Cassara* when we are naked. *Cristiano*, please. Shout it, sob it, scream it. All are acceptable. And all bear endless repeating, as I think you'll find soon enough."

And he was so close he could see her delicate shiver.

"How sure you seem that you won't be the one crying out my name." Julienne smirked at him. She actually dared *smirk* at him. "Particularly when we have yet to establish if there's the slightest bit of chemistry between us. Perhaps there will be nothing here but apologetic grimaces and embarrassment."

"My mistake," Cristiano said.

He didn't argue the point.

He moved closer and took her mouth with his.

No finesse. No gentility or politeness. Simple, potent greed.

He took what he wanted, a bold mating of lips and tongues. He tasted her, he took her, providing a comprehensive example of precisely the kind of demands he meant.

He didn't go easy on her at all.

And she met him, his Julienne. She pushed herself off the wall, twined herself around him, and the fire of it roared through him. The gut punch, hot and mad, slammed into him. It made him question the limits of his own control, when he prided himself on never, ever losing his grip—

When he pulled away, his own breath was hard to catch. Her eyes had gone dark and wide, and Cristiano wanted nothing on this earth but to bury himself inside her, again and again.

Assuming he lived through the single night he would allow her.

The single night he would allow *himself.*

And as he fought to find his control again, he wondered, for the first time in his life, if one night would be enough.

A sentiment that should have sent him reeling. Running for the hills, but her taste was in his mouth. Sweet and salt, all woman, and he thought it entirely possible that she might be the undoing of him, after all.

The mad part of it was, he couldn't seem to care.

"One night," he said again, rougher this time. Because he was talking to himself. "That's all I have to offer."

"All you have to offer me? Or all you have to offer, in general?"

He didn't know how she knew to ask him that.

But the grief was always in him, the shame his constant shadow, and he told himself that was what made him reach over and run his thumb over her full, tempting lower lip. He wanted to sink his teeth into her. He wanted to breathe her in, then get his mouth where she was sweetest.

"Does it matter?"

He watched her chest rise, then fall. He could see her nipples, tight and hard beneath the silk blouse she wore. He caught the faintest hint of her arousal and his mouth watered.

"One night," she agreed. Almost solemnly. But then she smiled. "But I hope you don't have performance anxiety. It would be depressing if you failed somehow to live up to all this hype."

He smiled then, edgy and wrong, and had the distinct pleasure of watching goose bumps break out all over her body.

"Let me worry about that. All you need to worry about is how many times you scream my name." He leaned closer and sampled the goose bumps on her neck, then smiled there, against her skin. "Remember it, please. *Cristiano*. Though in desperate circumstances *Oh, God* is also acceptable."

When all she did was pant a little, her eyes

glazed over with heat when he angled himself back to look at her, he laughed.

And then he took by the hand this woman who he intended to purge tonight, one way or the other. He led her out of the alcove, back to the lobby elevators, and then spirited her away to the penthouse suite he'd taken on the very top floor.

Where he intended to keep her until dawn.

Using every last scrap of the dark.

Until they were both fully sated.

And perhaps, at last, truly saved from the mistakes he'd made ten years ago.

CHAPTER THREE

THIS WAS WHAT she'd wanted.

Julienne's mouth felt beautifully tender. She pressed her fingertips against her lips as Cristiano ushered her into his hotel suite, sensation pulsing hot and raw from that point of contact all the way down to her toes.

She expected him to turn on the lights. Indulge in suitably urbane conversation, dry to match the cocktails. Or whatever it was men like him did in situations like these.

But instead, he kissed her again, barely getting the door closed before his mouth was on hers.

Dark. Hot.

So greedy it almost hurt.

And there was some part of her that couldn't quite believe that a man so controlled, so deeply ascetic, could carry all this passion within him. Could have been carrying it deep inside him somewhere, all this time.

But she couldn't care about that now. Not when his mouth was on hers and his hands roamed everywhere, finding her breasts and then taking possession of her nipples.

As if they were his.

As if *she* was his.

They were still in the entryway, though she hardly saw it. Or cared. She had the sense of more marble, more mirrors, and the pervasive sense of tremendous wealth—which was to say, nothing special in the Cassara world.

But his mouth was still on hers, beguiling her and bewildering her, and she stopped worrying about where they were. Only that he was with her.

Cristiano's hands were restless, moving where they pleased. One dove beneath the waistband of her skirt to find the curve of her bottom. The other drifted to her waist, then up, pushing her bra out of his way to hold her naked breast in his palm.

All the while he kissed her, intoxicating her. Making her press into him. Making her wish she could crawl inside him.

She had never understood the word *demanding* before. Not really.

Cristiano was overwhelming behind a desk. But here, unleashed…

He was like a hurricane.

He kissed her with a ferocity that should have terrified her. That might have, if it hadn't been for the sensation that howled and shook through her with every stroke of his hand, his tongue. She felt strung out between his taste and his touch. The insistent fingers on her breast and then, below, the way he traced his way over her bottom. And kept going until he found his way to her front, and the furrow of her molten heat.

And then he was inside her, two fingers deep into the center of her need.

A wicked twist, and then more of that unreal dark laughter against her mouth as she bucked into him. And moaned.

"My name," he murmured.

Another demand.

Then he pressed down hard, thrusting deep, and Julienne dissolved.

She heard a keening sound, but all she was conscious of were those thick, strong fingers inside of her—thrusting so wickedly, with such certainty and skill.

She sank from one peak only to find herself tossed up hard into another.

And all the while, Cristiano laughed.

Low, male, deeply satisfied.

But still, it was laughter. And Julienne wanted to hoard it. Gather it up and hold it close, for all those years she would have sworn to anyone who would listen that this man didn't know how to laugh. That he never had. That he simply wasn't made that way.

He pulled his fingers from the tight grip of her sex. Then, impossibly, he lifted them to his own mouth.

Julienne watched, torn somewhere between a sharp, hot longing and a crisp embarrassment as he licked his fingers clean.

"All this time." His voice was a wondering rasp. "All this time you sat across tables and desks from me. You've walked in and out of my offices on five continents. And all this time, you have tasted like this."

She felt as if she ought to apologize, though she couldn't quite speak. And her heart felt fragile and fierce at once, there where it swelled behind her ribs. Cristiano peeled her away from the wall and her knees wobbled beneath her when she meant to stand.

Her reward for that was that dark laugh of his again, a rough, masculine music she thought she would hear inside her forever.

Then he picked her up, tossing her over his shoulder with an easy strength that reminded her of the ancient conquerors who surely lived in his blood.

He strode through the darkened rooms of his hotel suite and she saw glimpses of bright lights heralding the Monte Carlo nightlife through the windows, gleaming antiques strewn about the palatial living spaces, and with every step, the quiet whisper of five-star luxury.

And when he put her down, he tipped her over onto her belly. Julienne tried to orient herself in the dimness of a new room, taking longer than she should have to recognize that he'd bent her over the side of a tall bed. And she tried to take stock, she did—but her body was his now. Not hers.

Never again yours, a voice said in her so clearly she almost flinched at the sound. *His always. His forever.*

And she could no longer tell if she was shuddering because of that voice, or because of him. Or some wicked, ruthless combination of both.

She felt him behind her, crouched down with a hand on one ankle, and all she could manage to do was moan.

"These legs," he said, in that same tone, like a dark incantation. "I worked so hard to keep myself from noticing these legs, Julienne. The temptation of them. And the shoes. Always the shoes, higher and higher by the year."

And all she could think was, *You weren't invisible to him after all.*

She almost felt herself shatter into pieces at that notion alone.

And then she was shivering all over, everywhere, as he slid his palms up the back of her legs. Not quite gently. Not quite softly. And the firm pressure was all about heat and want, making her delirious. Making her ripe and half-mad with that drumming desire.

It was only when he slid his hands down the length of her legs again that she realized he'd pushed up her skirt and left it bunched up at her waist.

She felt a wallop of that bright hot pulsing thing that had nearly knocked her over in the hall. It was mixed now with the image of what she must look like, bent over his bed in such a wanton display, with only the bright red thong she wore between them.

Julienne was breathing so hard now that it was all she could hear. That gasping thing not quite a breath, high and wild.

"Feel free to bite down on the linens," Cristiano told her, dark and amused. "I won't tell."

She didn't bite down. But she did grip the soft bedclothes beneath her, twisting the outrageously soft material into fists.

His fingers moved beneath her thong, almost absently, when she could *feel* the intensity coming off of him in waves. She felt him peel it down her leg, then tug it from one ankle. But not the other, and she understood—with another wallop—that he'd left her thong there.

How must she *look*…?

She was naked from the waist down, wearing only her impractical heels with her lacy red thong at one ankle. And she was making that *sound*. And his shoulders were between her legs, tipping her forward even more and lifting her at the same time, so she was braced even more fully on the bed—

"Oh, God," she moaned, as understanding slammed into her with all the force of a train.

"There you go," he murmured.

Approvingly.

And she could hear him well enough, but worse—or better—his mouth was *right there*. Right there at her core, where she felt herself clenching, melting, shuddering—

Then Cristiano took her in his mouth from behind, like an overripe peach.

And ate her like dessert.

And this time, when she exploded, she screamed.

Sometime later, he rolled her over. Julienne lay there, splayed wide, because she couldn't seem to get her limbs to work. Nor could she manage to care about that strange paralysis the way she knew she should.

All the while her heart clattered so hard against her ribs that she was worried they might crack. Or she would.

She had the vague sense that he was moving, but then he was touching her again. Stripping her, she worked out after a moment, with a ruthless efficiency that made her shiver all over again.

"Cristiano…" she murmured.

"Good girl," he replied.

She had no idea why that made her want to sob. Though she couldn't have said, if her life depended upon it, what sort of sob that might have been. Another explosion of sensation. Or a deep well of something that had ached inside her for much too long now, too fiercely to be sadness.

All of the above, she said to herself.

At least, she thought it was to herself. It was impossible to tell.

And then he was crawling over her, tasting her as he went.

No part of her was safe from him, and she felt blazingly hot. Gloriously alight and alive. She tasted him too, so male and hard. Until she was sure they both glowed in the dark with the force of this endless temptation, wild and needy.

She wanted it to go on and on forever.

And then she felt him, hard and huge against her hip.

She realized she must have made a noise when he laughed again, softly.

"You're going to take all of me, Julienne," he told her, with that quiet certainty that made her doubt—not for the first time—that she was really going to survive this. Not in one piece, anyway.

Not intact. But she'd known that before she'd come here, hadn't she? Not the particulars of *how*, exactly, he would ruin her. Only that he would. "Do you understand?"

All Julienne could do was nod. She didn't know if she was apprehensive, or desperate—but this time, in a whole new way. She wanted to prove to him that she could do exactly that. That she could do whatever he wanted, whatever he needed.

He smiled again, and it was even more devastating than before.

And she was such a fool. Had she really worried that the sight of his smile might make her swoon?

If only.

The sad truth of her situation was like another wallop, and now it was connected to that molten fire between her legs, the pounding of her heart, and the dark, demanding man propped up over her.

She had fallen hopelessly in love with this man when she was sixteen years old. She had loved him with all the mad fervency of a teenage girl, because she'd been one. And more, with the unwavering passion a girl could only have for the hero who had saved her.

It had never wavered. Over the years, it had grown stronger. Deeper.

Until even her own sister despaired of her.

Tonight was meant to be the cure. Because no

man could possibly live up to the fantasies in her head. Julienne knew that. She'd been sure of it.

And tonight was nothing like her fantasies, it was true.

Cristiano was far, far better than she ever could have imagined.

And she could see the vast gulf between the teenage crush she'd had on him all this time and the reality that was this. *Him.* His ruthless physicality. His rampant, commanding masculinity, his certainty in her responses and his dark demands.

God help her, but she was lost.

He thrust into her then, a slow and steady ruthlessness that had her coming apart at the feel of it. The thickness. That deep, aching stretch. The tug of it, there at her entrance, that he barely heeded.

Then the ruthless, peremptory way he seated himself deep inside her, looked down at her face and smiled.

Julienne shattered all around him. She loved him with every last inch of her woman's body, shattering what was left of her teenage heart and loving him all the more with the far darker, far more complicated adult heart that remained.

Fantasies were nothing next to this.

She shook and she shook, and she heard his name on her lips.

A song she'd already been singing for a decade, and would likely keep singing all the days of her life.

She told herself she accepted it. She *needed* to accept it.

Cristiano gathered him to her, laughing again. It was dark music to her ears, she buckled anew, and only then did he begin to move.

And Julienne lost track of the things she sobbed, or the times she screamed. He was insatiable, and he was thorough. He taught her things she was sure she could never put into words, so she used the only one that she could remember.

His name.

It could have been hours or whole lifetimes when he finally rolled her over for the last time, pulled her knees up high and let himself go.

And it was her name she heard then, roared out into the crook of her neck as he found his own release.

One more thing that she would hoard, later.

One more piece of treasure to tuck away.

He had said one night, and he used every last scrap of it.

Julienne woke as the first hint of dawn crept across the sky, and had no idea how she was supposed to go on. Not now she knew.

She'd come here to exorcise her own, personal

demons. And instead, she had lost herself all the more. Irrevocably.

But none of that mattered, because they had agreed.

One night.

"You need your own life," Fleurette had told her, time and again. "Not *his* life, his company, his world. You're not a princess locked away in a tower, waiting for some fool to ride up on a white horse. That's what Annette dreamed of, you know. Every time she went out. And look what happened."

Julienne had always agreed, safe in the knowledge that it was easy enough to agree with whatever Fleurette said as long as she still had to pay him back. And could therefore agree and also carry on doing what she was doing.

But she'd paid him back in full before she'd met him in the bar last night, transferring the last of the money to the account she'd set up for that purpose. He had bought her, in a sense, but she had bought herself back.

She was sure that once she recovered from this night—once she walked away from him, reminded herself how to breathe, and found her way into the new life she planned to build for herself far away from the Cassara Corporation or anything that reminded her of Monaco and the girl she'd been when she'd come here the first time—she would treasure that.

You will have to, she told herself, a new sob building inside her.

She twisted in the bed, looking over her shoulder to where Cristiano slept.

Even in sleep, he looked stern. Unyielding.

Both of which he'd proved himself to be, over and over again.

Julienne didn't let herself touch him again. Because she knew that if she did, she would never manage to tear herself away.

Instead she pressed one palm hard against her treacherous heart.

One night, he had said.

And any emotional complications she had were her own.

She made herself get up, then pull on her clothes. She picked up her shoes in one hand, then found her way out through the maze of rooms toward that entryway where he'd feasted on her like a wild thing.

Julienne shuddered all over again, instantly hot and wet and ready. She lectured herself as she looked in the mirror, dismayed to find that she did not look nearly as rumpled and used as she thought she should. Her hair was wild, but it was easily tamed. She smoothed it back, then tied it into a knot.

And then she looked the way she always did.

As if nothing had changed. As if she was somehow the same person she'd been when she'd walked in here last night.

When the truth was, she had saved herself for the only man she had ever looked at twice. The only man she had ever loved. She'd saved herself for him, and he had taken her as ruthlessly as he did everything, none the wiser.

And as she let herself out of the hotel room, closing the door quietly behind her, Julienne found herself smiling.

It was hardly on par with rescuing a sixteen-year-old girl from prostituting herself, but it was a gift in return for a gift all the same.

He had protected her innocence all those years ago. And last night she had joyfully, happily, given it to him.

"You can move on now," she told herself, ignoring the way her heart thudded so painfully in her chest. She leaned down to slip on one shoe, then the next. And she could still feel him everywhere, the rasp of his rough jaw on her inner thighs. His hard, gloriously male hands so big and bold against her skin. "It's over now, Julienne. You'll move on."

You will have to, came the voice inside, too much like her sister's.

And she made herself walk away—from Monaco, from her sordid past, from the Cassara Corporation, and from Cristiano himself—without looking back.

CHAPTER FOUR

Six months later

CRISTIANO SCOWLED DOWN at his mobile as he crossed the Piazza del Duomo, then shoved it into his pocket. It was a blustery spring evening in Milan, and he had no intention of answering the call coming in. Or any call, because he did not wish to risk getting sucked back into the latest set of fires he would be duty bound to extinguish tonight.

And tonight he had other plans. Tonight he thought he might spend some time in his home for a change. The glorious penthouse that was as sleek and modern and stark as he liked, with no hint of sweetness. No chocolate. And best of all, not in his office. He thought he might try his hand at pretending he was a real man with a real life, instead of the walking, talking embodiment of the Cassara Corporation.

He would never admit such a thing aloud, and

certainly not in a place like Milan where his grandfather had worked so very hard for so long and had admirers everywhere, but sometimes he wondered if he might not take a great deal of pleasure in watching it all burn.

Another vicious little thought that should have been unworthy of him. He filed that away with the rest of them, the evidence of who he really was no matter how he tried to pretend otherwise, and shoved his hands into the pockets of his coat.

As if he needed any more proof that he was his father's son, through and through.

Still, he collected each and every damning morsel himself. And kept a very thorough dossier, right there where his heart ought to be.

And he was thinking about all the ways he'd failed himself and his grandfather's memory again when he saw her.

One more thing he was sick of, he thought with an internal snarl, when the initial kick of it passed.

Cristiano loved women. He loved sex. And he indulged himself, one night at a time. He had never wanted more than one night with anyone. Ever.

And yet he had spent six months being haunted by that single night he'd spent with Julienne Boucher in Monaco.

He'd woken up that morning after to find Julienne gone, and had hated the fact that her absence hadn't brought him the usual peace or satisfaction.

Instead, he'd been forced to acknowledge the distinctly unsavory truth.

He, Cristiano Cassara, had wanted *more.*

Had he woken to find her still there in his bed, he would have broken every last one of his rules and indulged himself further.

It was unthinkable and unprecedented—but that didn't make the unfamiliar urge any less real.

He'd assured himself that the odd need in him he'd never felt before, that ravenous hunger, would fade. Give it a week's time, he'd told himself confidently as he'd left Monaco with no plans to return, and he would forget her like all the rest.

But he didn't.

He saw Julienne's face everywhere. A gleaming bit of caramel-colored hair and he was instantly distracted. The turn of a particular cheek, soft and elegant, and he trailed off in the middle of a sentence—no matter what he happened to be doing. Negotiating deals, handling problems, whatever.

She would not leave him alone, and yet she was nowhere to be found.

It was a nuisance. It was madness.

And it didn't fade with time.

Julienne's letter of resignation had been on his desk in Milan, as promised. She had left a dutiful forwarding address—the Manhattan residence she'd used throughout her tenure at the Cassara Corporation. But when, a month or so later, Cristiano had broken and actually attempted to contact her there, it turned out she'd moved on again.

This time, with no forwarding details.

She had turned into his own, personal ghost.

When Cristiano had never believed in ghosts before.

And so he scowled at the woman there in the *piazza*, wearing an overly bulky coat and an unnecessary scarf as if it was the dead of winter instead of April, because it wasn't her. It was never her.

Except this time, the caramel-haired woman in question held his gaze. And smiled back.

The bright red ribbon inside him that he'd been calling *self-loathing* brightened, then. And shifted into a new kind of fury.

He didn't know what else to call it.

Cristiano realized he had come to a complete stop. And was now standing perfectly still, his eyes locked to hers across the coming dusk. He was vaguely aware of the usual crowds that flocked to the *piazza*. Tourists and locals alike, gazing up at the ancient cathedral and taking photographs of its spires. But all he saw was Julienne.

That *smile*.

And, as he watched, it shifted from some kind of greeting, laced with hope if he had to characterize it, into that cool weapon he recalled from the bar in Monaco.

Either way, she made his body tighten into a hard, driving greed.

She was standing still herself, her gaze on him and that puffy down coat arranged around her like a circus tent.

It suggested to him that she'd been standing out here a long while.

Cristiano was moving then, cutting through the crowd, or perhaps it was simply that they leaped out of the way of a man with that much hunger on his face.

He kept his gaze trained on Julienne, half-convinced that if he so much as blinked she might disappear like smoke.

Then he was standing before her, astonished at the new kind of greed that swelled in him. He wanted to get his hands on her again—that hadn't changed—but it was more than that. For a moment, he was content simply to gaze at her.

Like a puppy, a cold voice inside him chimed in.

A voice he recognized, snide and sneering. Like Giacomo at his worst.

Cristiano clenched his jaw, fighting back the darker urges inside him, because that was the point, wasn't it? It wasn't the urges that mattered. It wasn't the part of him that could match his father's snideness all too easily. He knew those things existed. It was what he did with them that mattered, surely.

"Julienne," he made himself say, by way of greeting. As if this was a business meeting that required his cold ruthlessness, and had nothing to do with that *smile*. "There must be a reason you are lurking about out here in the elements. I'm astonished you felt the urge to play tourist on such a wet, cold evening."

"I'm an excellent tourist, actually," she replied, and he was sure he saw some trace of emotion in her toffee-colored eyes. Here a moment, then gone. "But that's not why I'm here."

"Dare I flatter myself that you have come back to Milan to see me?" He couldn't help the iciness in his tone. The frigid bite of it. Maybe he didn't want to help himself. "You know where the Cassara offices are located, do you not? And last I checked you knew where my residence was located as well. Surely either choice would be more appropriate than stalking me in the shadow of the Duomo."

"I've been waiting for you, Mr. Cassara. Not stalking you."

"Have we reverted, then, to Mr. Cassara? Fascinating. I had my mouth between your legs, *cara*. Surely that buys a man some measure of intimacy."

"I didn't want to presume."

She sounded prim, but there was heat on her cheeks. And the oddest notion occurred to him, then. Could it be that his favorite ice queen was

less cool and unbothered than she looked? How...
delightful.

He didn't really want to think too hard about
how delightful he found it. Because that brought
him right back to snide commentary from a dead
man.

"I told you what name to use," he said quietly
now, his gaze on hers while the night they'd shared
played in his head. "You may sob it again, if you
wish. If that makes you more comfortable."

"I need a moment of your time, that's all," she
said. Almost formally. But then there was that heat
on her cheeks again, brighter than before, and he
wondered what images she played in her head.
"Not your name."

Cristiano lifted his hands and spread them wide,
in keeping with a casualness he in no way felt. "I
have nothing but time, naturally. I am a man of
leisure, capable at any moment of playing tourist
in my own city."

She blinked at that, her cheeks reddened further,
and he got the distinct impression that she'd expected him to put up a fight. That she was braced
for it.

"You're not the only one interested in another
taste, Julienne," he said, feeling magnanimous.
Because she was here, finally. Because it wasn't
yet another ghost to haunt him and distract him,
whether he believed in ghosts or not. It was her,

this time. It was finally *her.* "I tried to find you in Manhattan, but you'd moved."

She coughed, as if to cover a sound of shock. "You came to Manhattan?"

He arched a brow. "I often have business in Manhattan. As you are well aware."

But there was a different, softer light in her gaze. "Yes, right. You didn't make a special trip. I understand." She smiled at him and he didn't know how he kept his hands off her. "It was my sister's turn, you see."

"Her turn?"

A fresh flush made her cheeks glow. "I can't imagine why you'd be interested in this story."

"Her turn to do what?" Cristiano inquired silkily. "I trust it will not involve any Monte Carlo reenactments."

"God. No." She seemed to hear her own vehemence then, and looked away, that belligerent chin of hers firming. "Ever since you rescued us that night, we followed my path through the Cassara Corporation because it was the fastest way to meet our goals. To repay you and reclaim our lives. But once I resigned, it was time to follow Fleurette's path. It's only fair."

"Why must you choose? Why can't you both do as you like instead of hiding away so theatrically?"

It was only after he asked the question, out here as the moody spring night drew close, that Cristiano thought to question why on earth it was he was standing about having random conversations with this woman. When he'd spent six months dreaming of all the other things he could do with her. With her mouth. With every square inch of her delectable body. With that heat he could feel between them even now. Even though they weren't touching.

"That was the deal we made ten years ago," Julienne said, stoutly. "And I didn't imagine anyone would be looking for me after my resignation or I would have left my forwarding details, with no theater whatsoever. We're in Seattle now."

"Seattle." He pronounced the name of the American city as if it might bite. "That is off to the west, is it not?"

"The Pacific Northwest, actually."

"You will forgive me if I do not spend a great amount of time tramping about the primeval forests of the American northwest, Pacific or otherwise," Cristiano said, his voice going edgy despite his best efforts. "As I traffic neither in legacy technology nor flannel shirts."

"I don't recall asking you for a review of Seattle's charms," Julienne said, with a smile he realized was fixed. "I'm merely telling you that we moved. And time passed."

"That is what time does." His jaw was tight. And impatience beat in him, hard and hot. "Have you turned up in the *piazza* to tell me bedtime stories, *cara*? If I'm a good boy, will you provide me with warm milk and a pat on the head? You will understand if I decline the kind offer, I hope."

He watched her straighten her shoulders. Then that chin of hers tipped up. "My sister wants me to have nothing to do with you or Cassara chocolates ever again. She claims she is the practical one, you understand, but it's actually because she cannot bear to think about where we came from. If she could, I think she would wipe Monaco from the map entirely. To say nothing of that hill town where we were born."

"I find the emotional travails of your sister at least as interesting as the story of your domestic arrangements. In case you wondered."

"She argued strenuously against my coming here."

"Had you reached out to me, I would have offered a counterargument." Because she kept talking, and all he could concentrate on was her mouth.

"Cristiano—" she began.

"First, the counterargument, if you please."

And he indulged himself, because he no longer had the strength to hold himself back. Or the will. Or the slightest inclination.

Cristiano reached over, taking his time as he slid his palm along her jawline to cup her cheek.

Because he wanted to feel her silky softness. And her heat.

Her breath fanned out, half a gasp and half something else. It was like music to him.

And her eyes were sweet like candy, if darker tonight. Dark enough to remind him of the precise shade they'd been when he'd been deep inside of her. He felt himself harden, until his need was more like an ache.

He felt those iron chains he kept locked tight around him, to keep all his compartments in a tidy order, snap open—but not as if she'd broken them.

It was as if she was the key.

And Cristiano couldn't allow himself to think about that.

Instead, he leaned forward and nipped at that lower lip of hers, full and tempting.

And maybe she said his name. He couldn't tell because his blood was roaring in his ears, and the faintest taste of her was enough to make his whole body clench tight.

He bent again, and covered her mouth with his.

And on some level he expected it to be a disappointment. Because no kiss could possibly live up to his memories. He had exaggerated her taste. Her fit. He expected to find that he'd sold himself a fantasy no reality could ever match.

But instead, Julienne took the top of his head off.

He forgot where they were. He forgot the crowd,

the weather. The ancient cathedral that blocked out the better part of the sky.

All of that was so much dust in the wind to him, because Julienne was kissing him again, and it was better than anything Cristiano could possibly have remembered.

It was better.

It was her.

He swept her into his arms like the romantic he had never been, tilting her back so he could take more, taste more, lose himself more—

And it was only when he heard the high-pitched tittering sound of a set of teenage girls nearby that reality reasserted itself.

"Dio santo!" he growled furiously, there against her mouth. "What have you done to me, woman?"

But Julienne pulled back, stepping out of his embrace. And the expression he saw on her face made no sense at all, because she looked… stricken. More, she'd gone pale, leaving only two bright splotches on those cheekbones of hers, like flags.

"I'm afraid my sister was right." Her voice was husky. Distressed. "I shouldn't have come here."

"Indeed not," he agreed. "You should have found me somewhere private, so I could greet you properly. And without risk of arrest."

And he watched her change again, a sweep of pink taking over her face as if she'd leaped from an ice bath into a furnace. She even laughed a little, fanning at her face while she did.

"You're overheating, Julienne," he said shortly. "It is obviously that ridiculous coat."

Cristiano reached over, grasped the zipper that she'd tugged up to just beneath her chin, and pulled it loose.

And later, he would remember that she'd made a noise. That her arms came up as if to ward him off.

Here, now, he watched her mouth drop open. He watched her eyes darken, just the way he liked them. And then his gaze dropped down to trace the curves of that body he'd learned in such exquisite detail that their single night together was branded forever into his mind.

His first thought was that she must have augmented her breasts, however little that made sense with what he knew of her, because they were bigger. Rounder and plumper, which made his mouth water. His palms itch.

And his gaze moved lower still, to take her all in—

But he stopped.

Because his mind simply refused to make sense of what he saw.

Worse, what it meant.

The bells of the city began to ring out the hour. Eight strikes, and each one like a poisoned spear thrust deep into his chest.

Her hands crept up and covered her belly, but it was too late. And her hands were too small.

Because Julienne Boucher had a giant belly. It was big, round and unmistakably pregnant.

Six months, something in him intoned. *Six. Months.*

Cristiano could not comprehend it.

He could not do more than stare.

"I didn't know for a long time," Julienne told him, hurriedly, though he wasn't sure he could make sense of her words. Or anything outside of that lurching in him. That great, deep howl. "I wasn't ill, you see. I was fairly fatigued, that's all. But a bit of fatigue seemed like a reasonable response to working as hard as I've done for the past ten years. Or to what happened in Monte Carlo, even. And then there was the move out west and all the details of setting up a new life. All of those things are fatiguing, are they not?"

She was talking too fast. And he kept staring at that belly of hers, that enormous belly.

Where she carried a child.

Where she carried *his—*

But he couldn't go there. His entire body and mind rejected it.

Julienne was still talking, her words tripping over each other. "When my clothes stopped fitting, I assumed it was because I was finally relaxing. Enjoying my food and no longer desperate to keep up appearances, always pretending I had nothing in common with that trashy little wannabe tramp who found you in Monte Carlo all those years ago. I congratulated myself on letting go, at last."

Was that what she expected? His congratulations?

Cristiano's throat worked, but he could not seem to produce a sound.

"So I didn't understand until quite late," she told him, her gaze wide and solemn. "A month ago, maybe six weeks, I happened to get out of the bath and look at myself in a mirror sideways. And then I began to count back."

"Six months," Cristiano said, as if from a great distance, and across the great desert of that howling thing in him.

"Six months," Julienne agreed. She cleared her throat. "And I want to make something perfectly clear, Cristiano. This was not my intention. This was never my intention. I wanted the bookends we spoke of that night, nothing more. You owe me nothing."

All he could do was stare at her. Not a ghost tonight. Not a common haunt, a memory he couldn't shake.

But his own, personal demon, come to destroy him.

"I'm here because I thought it was the right thing to do. To tell you, I mean, but you should feel no sense of obligation. I truly mean that. Fleurette doesn't think I need to tell you at all, but I know you are an honorable man. You have always been an honorable man. And I felt certain that you would wish to know, even if you don't—"

The howling thing inside him stopped. But behind it was something far blacker. His rage.

He lifted his gaze to meet hers, his eyes like fire, and Julienne stopped talking.

Abruptly.

As if he'd slapped her.

Cristiano had never slapped a woman in his life, but in that moment, the chaos in him had control. And he could not have said what he might do next. He was a man allergic to uncertainty, and yet he had *no idea*.

"Cristiano," she began, carefully.

"You have said enough, I think."

He hardly recognized his own voice. It was stark. Harsh. As gray and cold as the city all around them. And inside him, the guilt and the shame that had always lurked there, waiting, rose up like the tide. Sweeping him under at last, then dragging him out to sea.

And that was the trouble with shame. With guilt. It only felt like drowning when the harder truth was he lived on. Despite everything, he lived on.

"Cristiano. Please." Julienne's eyes took on a particular sheen that some part of him recognized as tears. An emotion he did not wish to name.

He was far past that.

Out in that cold sea, going under, far away from any land.

"I will never forgive you for this," he told her, whole winters on his face. In his soul. And that terrible sea that choked him in his voice. "Mark my words, Julienne. I will never forgive you."

CHAPTER FIVE

THERE WAS SOMETHING raw and frozen in his gaze, and Julienne's chest hurt as if she'd breathed in too deep on a frigid morning, but Cristiano did not say anything further. Not to her.

He made two terse phone calls in a clipped, dark tone, then ushered her back across the *piazza*, his long, athletic stride giving her no quarter.

But it didn't occur to her not to go with him.

She didn't know what she'd been expecting, if she was honest with herself. Him to cry out in joy? Gather her into an embrace and dance around the *piazza*, like one of those strange American commercials for prescription medication?

"He will hate you," Fleurette had said, a judge handing down a verdict. "He will hate you, he will hate the baby, and I cannot see why it's the moral thing to do to subject either one of you to him. You repaid him already, Julienne. You do not owe him anything else. Ever."

She had not wanted to believe her sister.

More than that, she could admit—with a creeping sense of shame that bloomed all the brighter as he marched her to a waiting car, then bundled her into the back—she had wanted...

This, she supposed. Whatever *this* looked like.

Maybe all she'd wanted was to see him again. And this particular excuse to see him again was unassailable, whether he forgave her or not. She wasn't seeking his forgiveness. She was having his child.

And she would have to live with the part of her that exulted in that, and not because there was a life inside her that she was already desperately, hopelessly in love with. Or not *only* that. There was also the part of her that took far too much pleasure in the notion that their lives would forevermore be tangled together now, hers and Cristiano's, no matter what reaction he had to her pregnancy.

Julienne was certain that a better person would not feel such things. A good mother would be focused on the baby and not on her own treacherous heart. But as hard as she tried to expunge herself of such self-interested, foolish emotion, it remained.

Taunting her.

Making her wonder if he knew—and if that was why he couldn't forgive her. God knew she wasn't sure she could forgive herself, either.

Julienne did not ask where they were headed.

He did not offer the information. They sat in the backseat of the car, separated by a few tense inches and a vast, unconquerable gulf of the fury that came off him in thick waves.

But she recognized the building they arrived at, sometime later. It was the house where she and Fleurette had lived in those first years after Monte Carlo, only leaving when Julienne had gotten her first real job at in the Cassara Corporation's UK office.

She shot him a sharp look as he ushered her out of the car and into the old house, but his face was closed down tight. Unreadable, save for that black, cold thing.

And Julienne understood that this was not a trip down memory lane when she saw the men waiting for them in the kitchen.

"I am a doctor," the oldest of the men said, smiling slightly while his white hair gleamed. "I believe I once treated you for bronchitis."

"Of course," Julienne murmured politely, feeling faintly ridiculous. She had no memory of having bronchitis or meeting any doctors, but then, that first six months or so after Cristiano had rescued them from Monte Carlo remained a blessed blur, even now.

The old man nodded. "If you'll come with me...?"

And it was not until the examination was done—until the necessary samples were taken and

Julienne was dressed and sitting in the old living room that she had once believed was the very pinnacle of style and luxury—that she accepted the fact that Cristiano had hurt her feelings.

"You're being ridiculous," she muttered to herself, glaring down at her hands as she wound them together over the very crest of her bump. "He cannot take your word for it. How many women must turn up with paternity claims? He would be a fool if he did not verify this personally."

And if she knew anything about Cristiano Cassara, it was that he was never a fool.

That didn't make her feelings hurt any less, but it felt better to think about things practically. No matter how impractical she might feel on the inside.

Her mobile buzzed in her pocket and she pulled it out, not surprised to see that she'd missed a host of messages from Fleurette.

Did you tell him?

Was it terrible?

Are you okay?

She texted back.

I told him. He is confirming paternity.

And she slid her phone back in her pocket and muted it, because she knew too well what her sister's response to that would be.

After what seemed to her like a very long time, sitting there in silence in a house that was no longer hers—and had never been hers, if she was honest, or ever felt like more than the gift it had always been that she'd tried so hard to earn—she heard a noise at the door.

Julienne knew all she needed to about herself when her heart leaped at the notion that it might be him.

It wasn't.

"Have you booked into a hotel, Ms. Boucher?" the man who stood there asked with a certain level of calm deference, as if Julienne might not recall that this was Massimo, Cristiano's secretary.

And Massimo was perfectly polite, as always. There was no reason for Julienne to interpret his question as aggressive. Or snide in some way.

Don't go making intrigue when there is only inquiry, she cautioned herself.

She named the hotel she'd checked into this morning, feeling outside herself as Massimo nodded, then withdrew.

And she was staring at her hands again when she felt the air change.

Because he didn't make a sound. Not one single sound.

There was that sense of some sort of disturbance, that was all. The hair on the back of her neck prickled. And Cristiano was there when she looked up, filling the doorway that led to the rest of the house and staring at her with that same raw fury making his dark eyes burn.

There were so many things she ought to have said. Julienne struggled to find the right words, but her tongue felt stiff. Heavy.

She realized then that she could still taste him on her tongue. That he could likely taste her, too.

Somehow, that made it all worse.

Her throat was tight. She couldn't tell if it was a sob or a scream. Or merely his name again.

And she understood as she stared back at him mutely that she'd been wrong about him all this time. Because she remembered him across all those years before that night in his hotel room in Monte Carlo. She remembered how cold and remote she'd thought him then. Always.

But she realized that he had not been cold at all.

Because now it was as if he was a block of frozen granite encased in sheets of ice.

His dark, bittersweet eyes glittered, but that was the only suggestion of heat she could see in him.

Everything else was ice. And the tension between them.

Taut. Harsh.

Julienne almost wished that he would say something. *Do* something. Even if it was terrible. Anything had to be better than this horrible silence.

She made herself swallow, though she felt as if there were knives in her throat. Perhaps actual knives would have been an improvement.

She swallowed again. Then cleared her throat. "If this situation is as terrible for you as it appears to be, I have a solution. I am perfectly happy to raise—"

"I would strongly suggest that you not finish that thought," Cristiano belted out, and she wished, then, that she had not been so desperate for him to speak.

Because it was worse when he did. His voice was so frigid she felt...chapped. And more, as if she was shaking apart at the seams, though it all seemed to be entirely inside her. As if she was built on a flimsy foundation that could tip over at the slightest provocation.

As if she had already, the longer he trained that pitch-dark gaze of his on her.

"You are carrying my child," he said, and there was no crack in his voice. No chink in the forbidding sheet of armor where his face should have been. Granite and ice. Ice and granite. "A boy."

"I know I am, thank you." Julienne forced a smile. "That's why I'm here, Cristiano."

"How could this happen?" he bit out. "And I would advise you not to get cute with me, Julienne. I understand the mechanics. But we used protection."

"Did we?" She sucked in a breath when his expression got, if possible, more forbidding. "That is to say, I can't claim that I was paying the slightest bit of attention."

His gaze was like flint. "I always use protection."

"So did my mother, as she liked to tell the world after a few drinks," Julienne said, with perhaps more flippant dark humor than necessary. "And yet here Fleurette and I are."

"What did you use?" he demanded. "Surely between the two of us, this should have been impossible."

"Whether it should have been impossible or not, it happened. Six months ago. It isn't going anywhere. *He* isn't going anywhere." But the way he was glaring at her seemed tinged with a kind of outrage, as if she'd done this to him. Deliberately. She blew out a breath. "And I was not using anything."

"Do you have habit of propositioning men, hoping they take care of the practicalities, and then failing to pay attention either way?"

"I don't have habit of men," she retorted, not sure where this wellspring of dark humor had come from. But she laughed anyway. "There has only ever been the one."

She saw his head tilt to the side, barely.
Barely.

And still, it was as if the room around them burst into flame.

Good job, Julienne, she snapped at herself. *Remember how you weren't going to tell him that? Ever?*

Across from her, Cristiano had gone glacial. "I beg your pardon?"

Julienne winced. She'd never wanted to tell him this truth. She'd never *planned* to tell him anything. He hadn't seemed to notice that night, and she'd assumed she'd never see him again. No need to burden him with the knowledge that he'd taken her virginity.

That was something she could hoard for herself. Like treasure.

But she rested her hands on the great roundness of her belly as she stared at him, so harsh and so bitterly cold, and really, what was the point of keeping these foolish secrets? What could any of it matter now?

"You do not habitually proposition men, is that what you're telling me?" he asked when she did nothing but gaze at him, and it was more knives then, slicing deep.

"I do not. Habitually or otherwise."

The tension between them rose even higher.

She could hear it pressing against her ears. Making her head ache.

"I don't really know how to answer that," she continued brightly. "Perhaps I'll begin a habit of propositioning men, now that I am involved in so many new things." She rubbed her belly, and somehow found herself smiling at him over the child they'd made. The *child*. She forgave him his response because she wasn't exactly at peace with it herself. How could she blame him? "You were the first. And yes, before you ask. The first proposition. The first man. The first father to my first baby."

A terrible storm moved over his face, though his only physical reaction was the way his jaw worked. He looked away then, and she watched him press his finger and thumb to either side of his nose.

Fighting back something. She told herself she was glad.

But she found she was breathing far too heavily anyway.

"Very well then," he said after a long while, like a man facing the gallows. "It is done."

Julienne could still feel that shaking thing, making her feel fluttery inside in all the wrong ways. But she made herself laugh anyway.

"It's a baby, Cristiano. Not a harbinger of the end of days."

It seemed to take him a lifetime for him to turn

his head back to her. And she wished he hadn't when that dark gaze of his landed on her with the weight of a great stone. Pressing the air from her lungs. Pressing the laughter out of her as if it had never been.

"I'm thrilled you find this so entertaining," he said, every syllable an accusation. More than an accusation, a verdict. And if a man's gaze could be a prison, she was sure she could see the metal doors clang shut all around her. Trapping her there in all that condemnation and cold. "I had no intention of continuing the Cassara bloodline."

Her mouth was dry while curiously, her palms were damp. "Surely continuing the bloodline is the first and foremost responsibility of a man of your position."

"Not for me." Again, that muscle in his jaw told her long, involved stories about how furious he was without him having to say a word. "My grandfather had two sons. One of them was by all accounts a good man, a credit to my grandfather, and an excellent steward of both the Cassara name and fortune. The other was my father. Miserable. Vicious. And deeply committed only to the bottle, never his family. Never his responsibilities. My uncle died in his twenties in a boating accident, taking my grandfather's dearest dreams with him. That left my father as the heir. To say that he was unable to live up to the expectations placed upon him would be to greatly understate the case."

He shook his head, but it looked like fury to Julienne, not sadness or loss, or even disappointment. "He bullied my mother. He would have treated me worse, had my grandfather not taken me in hand. But I vowed to myself a long time ago that it would end with me. I would never, ever take the risk that I would produce more Cassaras like my father."

"Then we won't." Julienne lifted her chin as she stared back at him. "This baby has just as much a chance to be a saint like your uncle as it does to turn out like your father."

"If you knew my father, you would understand that the risk is unacceptable."

"No one is born bad, Cristiano. They're made that way. The good news is, that means we can do our best to make sure we go in the opposite direction."

"Let us be clear what is at stake in this," Cristiano said darkly. "It is not simply a fortune. A corporation. The world is filled with both. It is also all the lives that hang in the balance of those things. Do you know how many people I employ? If I had been a man like my father, they all would have been ruined years ago. And you should be aware, Julienne, that I am more like my father than you would ever wish to know."

"That's ridiculous—" she began.

"A good man would never have touched you," he gritted out. "Much less the way I touched you, no matter what invitations you offered me after so many years. There is a darkness in me. There always has been, but you… You bring it out. And I can tell you from my experience with my own parents that such a darkness is no place to raise a child."

Her throat hurt again, and she had the sudden, terrible fear that it was tears waiting there, threatening to come out.

"I've already told you this, but you don't have to be involved," she managed to say, trying not to let her voice sound so thick. So obvious. And ignoring that sharp, stabbing sort of pain in her heart. "No one need ever know you have a son but you and me. I will take this baby away and raise him in Seattle, where he will grow up wrapped in flannel and immersed in technology, and who knows? Perhaps he will never come to Italy at all. It will be like it never happened."

And she could see that life stretch out before her, bright in its way and good, too—because she and Fleurette would care for this baby. They would devote themselves to him. They would do what they could to make sure he wanted for nothing.

But that sharp thing in her chest made it clear that wasn't the life she wanted. For her or the baby.

How had she managed to hide that from herself before now?

"I'm afraid that is impossible." And for a moment, Julienne could almost have sworn that the expression on Cristiano's face was that sadness, that loss, she'd been searching for before. "I don't know what you were expecting when you came here. But I will tell you now how it will be."

A kind of foreboding struck at her then, turning over inside her like a hot spike of pain. Of heat. Of something in between the two she wasn't sure she could name. "You don't get to decide how it will be."

His lips moved into something wholly mirthless, and darker than before. "My grandfather has an estate in Tuscany. It is quite remote, and will be a more than suitable place for you during your confinement."

"My...what did you say? My *what*?"

"I still don't know what you meant about your sister and you taking turns, but if that means that she must remain in Seattle, so be it. I'm not convinced that I care for her influence over you anyway."

Julienne let out something like a laugh. "You must have lost your mind."

"We already know that you have a habit of disappearing, Julienne." Those dark eyes glittered.

"You will go to Tuscany. You will have the baby. And the two of you will remain there."

She was panting, her heart punching hard in her chest, but when he only gazed back at her as if what he'd said was perfectly reasonable, she found herself laughing again. In amazement.

"And how long will we remain there? The rest of our lives?"

His eyes glittered, glacial and harsh. "I can't say."

"You can't say because it's absurd. You can't really think that I'm going to let you hide me away somewhere. I have no desire to raise my child in a prison, thank you. Even one in scenic Tuscany."

"I'm afraid you will find that is not up to you to *let me* do anything," he replied, too softly "It is done."

She shot to her feet, cursing her new, pregnant body and how unsteady it made her feel on her own feet. And now the trembling inside of her had spread to the rest of her limbs. Now she simply shook, and there was no way he didn't see it.

He saw it, all right. What was clear was that he didn't care.

"This is not the stone age, Cristiano. What you're talking about is illegal. Kidnap. False imprisonment. Do you want me to go on?"

"You're welcome to put your complaint in writing, of course." His gaze was impassive. His expression like stone. "You are no longer employed by the company and can therefore claim no access to the human resources department, but I'll be certain to read any complaint of yours as closely as it deserves."

He only watched her as she gaped at him, and she couldn't help another incredulous laugh. "I'm not going to go with you, Cristiano. I will never, ever sign up to be locked away in some tower in the middle of nowhere, with or without my baby."

"Do you have an alternative?" he asked her quietly, that glittering thing in his gaze a weapon. And he'd hit his mark, dead center. "Ask yourself this, please. Can you run from me? And if you do, do you truly believe I will not catch you?"

"Cristiano…" she whispered, though she had the terrible feeling it was already too late.

And that his name was less a song on her lips tonight than it had been once.

Especially when his mouth moved into that grim, hard line. "The question is not whether or not I can do what I wish. It is not even whether or not I should. The question is, Julienne, what can you possibly do to stop me?"

CHAPTER SIX

THE VILLA CASSARA was as beautiful as it was quietly renowned. It was a triumph of Italian country glory set down to make the most of the gentle Tuscan hills where, it was rumored, Cassaras had dreamed of sweet things for many generations.

Julienne had been a little too aware of the difference between reality and corporate marketing after all her years as a glorified candy seller, but that didn't make the Cassara family home any less impressive. If she'd been an invited guest, she would no doubt have called the place a paradise.

But the villa wasn't hers for a holiday. It was a prison. And it didn't matter how beautiful a prison was. What mattered was that she couldn't leave it as she chose.

Julienne had succumbed with embarrassingly little trouble. Cristiano had been implacable, as ever, but worse—he'd been correct. She could not outrun him. She certainly couldn't fight him off.

She was six months pregnant and more debilitating by far, she had lost her heart to him a long time ago.

And so she had clung to what shreds of dignity she had remaining. She had let him march her out of the house where she and Fleurette had once lived—where she had made him into a myth in her head. A legend of all that was good and right, when maybe that had been nothing but a fairy tale a lost girl told herself as she figured out how to find her way out of her own dark woods.

She rather thought it said unfortunate things about her that she felt more grief over the loss of her made-up version of Cristiano than she did about the fact he handed her into another car, escorted her to the Cassara Corporation offices, then took her to the roof where the Duomo rose in the distance. There he'd strapped her into his waiting helicopter.

Her priorities had shifted around when he hadn't boarded the helicopter himself, but let her fly away with his staff instead. She'd had nothing to do but think about the appropriate things to grieve as they flew through the night, away from the lights of Milan, then south toward Florence and the Tuscan countryside.

In the dark, as the helicopter came in to land, it was entirely too easy to see that there was absolutely nothing rolling out in all directions. Nothing but a vast inky black stretch, with only the villa casting off light, a small bright beacon in all the dark.

Her first, panicked assessment had not been wrong.

The next morning, Julienne had woken up in the room that the smiling housekeeper had escorted her to the night before. The room could easily have starred in a magazine spread on the wonders of Italian villas. Outside her windows, it didn't look any more real. It was a glorious stretch of pretty fields toward the horizon, the view studded with cypress trees, red poppies and purples wisteria.

But Julienne wasn't here to marvel at the pretty land and gardens. She was here against her will.

"You need to remember that," she told herself sternly.

The villa sat at the crest of a hill and no matter how high she climbed or how far she looked or walked in any direction, there was nothing. No other villas. No adorable Italian villages, tucked charmingly away beyond this hill or that.

Even if there hadn't been evident security, there to patrol the boundaries of the Cassara estate, it wasn't as if she could simply walk off and expect to get away. The estate didn't appear on any maps. It was so resolutely unmappable, in fact, that her mobile kept suggesting she was in the center of Florence.

She might have set off anyway, because Italy had been populated for thousands of years and she was bound to find *someone* if she walked far enough, but it wasn't just her she had to think about these days. And she didn't feel she could risk herself when she had the baby to consider.

It turned out that she could spend a lot of time brooding about that, too.

But it wasn't until later that first day that she truly realized exactly what it was that Cristiano had planned for her.

There was staff, but they only nodded and excused themselves. It became clear very quickly that they'd been instructed not to speak to her. Hours later, she found herself standing on one of the many patios, staring out at fields as the fog rolled in.

It was beautiful. And it was also…empty. No cars, no traffic. No signs of life. No indication that there was anything here, or anywhere near, but her.

Isolation to go along with her imprisonment, she understood then. Not just prison, but solitary confinement.

"You cannot expect me to live like this," she told him over the phone when she called him, shortly after that unpleasant revelation. "How can you remain in Milan, leaving me to molder away out in these fields?"

"Stranded in the prettiest prison on earth." His

voice was a dark rasp that should have horrified her. It didn't. "My heart bleeds."

"I've lived in cities almost all my life." Because the oppressive silence of the hill town she'd grown up in haunted her still. The only sound had been the wind. And the endless judgment of the citizens. But she didn't tell him that. She hardly liked admitting it to herself. "Do you really think I will take to the pastoral experience? I'll explode if I stay here."

"There is no *if*, Julienne." His voice was glacial. As immovable as he was. "You will stay right where you are. Your every need is attended to and who knows? Perhaps a spot of quiet contemplation will do you some good."

"And what of you?" she snapped back at him, gripping her mobile so tightly she was surprised it didn't snap in half. "Do you plan to live your life as if you don't have a woman and a baby hidden away out here like some syphilitic eighteenth century nobleman?"

"Enjoy the fresh air," he growled at her. "Indulge in la dolce vita. You are at the Villa Cassara, after all. The sweet life is guaranteed."

And it was only when he'd rung off that it occurred to her that really, he hadn't had to take her furious call in the first place. It wasn't as if the grand head of the Cassara Corporation answered his own phone, unless he wished it.

If he wanted to truly isolate her, if he wanted to keep her caged up here, there wasn't a single thing she could do about it unless she wanted to call the police.

Assuming there were police to call, this far away from anywhere.

Julienne wasn't proud of herself for crying, but she couldn't stop. Not for days, off and on. She blamed her hormones. But then, as one week ticked over into the next, something else kicked in.

She was a survivor, after all. She'd survived her beginnings in France, which was more than some could claim, her own poor, lost mother among them. And she hadn't accidentally survived it. She'd been prepared to do the unthinkable to rescue herself from that life. It made her stomach hurt to think of it now, but if Cristiano hadn't been sitting at that bar in Monte Carlo, someone else would have been. Some other man.

And Julienne would have done what she needed to do.

That thought often brought her shame. But now, left to her own devices in her lovely Tuscan prison, she decided instead to think of it as a strength.

She would do what she needed to do, because she always did.

Because that was who she was.

In this case, stranded here as she was, she had to accept that there was no way out. Unless she wanted to pull off an elaborate scheme that would involve stealing one of the vehicles—and behaving as if she wasn't pregnant. Maybe it would come to that, but first, she thought she'd try something else.

She'd always been extraordinarily good at doing her research. This had been a Cassara residence for generations. What she needed to do was gather as much information as possible where she was, and see where it led her.

And the more information, the better.

Because she intended to use it as a weapon.

"What do you mean, 'there are reporters'?" Cristiano asked in icy disbelief.

His secretary stood on the other side of the large desk and...quailed. When Massimo was normally unflappable. It was his superpower, in fact. Cristiano couldn't say that he liked the evidence that even the dependably immovable Massimo could look anything but in total control of all things, all the time.

Julienne, a voice inside him said. Foreboding, perhaps. Or simply a warning.

Because it couldn't be anything else.

"From what I can gather, sir, there are some questions about your grandfather's relationship with a woman," Massimo said, his face studiously blank. "A woman not your grandmother."

Cristiano ground his teeth together, but could not bring himself to speak.

Maybe that was a good thing.

Massimo gazed back at him as if, given his preference, he would have chopped off his own head rather than said such a thing. "I'm only repeating what the great mess of them had been shouting down in the lobby."

"The *mess* of them," Cristiano repeated. He had to fight for every scrap of advertising space across all media, but a whisper of scandal brought the vultures out in spades. But then, this was something he knew all too well after a lifetime as his father's son.

Cristiano wanted to do some shouting of his own. But he refrained.

Barely.

"They want to ask you questions about your grandparents, I believe," Massimo said apologetically. "And also, I'm afraid, about Sofia Tomasi."

Sofia Tomasi. A name Cristiano had hoped never to hear again.

His grandfather had died five years ago. Piero Cassara had personally built on an ancient Italian fortune to create Cassara Chocolates, the finest luxury chocolate brand in the world. And he had been a man of honor. So claimed the papers, his employees, even his rivals. Anything Cristiano knew about being a man—and not a sad example of one—he'd learned from his grandfather.

But his private life had been somewhat less sweet than the family business, particularly when thrust under the lens of public perception.

Cristiano wanted nothing to do with his grandmother, a bitter, dour old woman who still lived in a corner of the Tuscany estate, cared only for her own company, and was happy to tell anyone who asked that she'd turned her back on her husband, her marriage and her family long ago. Before Cristiano's uncle had died, in fact.

That she had never cared for her husband was an accepted fact of the Cassara storyline. Her parents had pressured her into marrying him, she'd done her duty, and once her two sons were born she'd wanted nothing to do with any Cassaras ever again. Cristiano had long imagined her his own, personal fairy-tale witch—hunkered down in a cottage on the edge of the property, bristling with malevolence anytime he ventured near.

He'd thought nothing of it. Just as he'd thought nothing of Sofia Tomasi, the woman his grandfather had called any number of things over the years. Housekeeper. Friend. Companion.

Mistress, Cristiano thought now.

Though the tabloids would start using much worse words, now they knew.

He supposed he'd always known what she was

to his grandfather. Like his grandmother, it wasn't a story that bore repeating. It was simply a fact. Accordingly, no one had commented on the relationship in years, at least not in Cristiano's hearing. Because everyone already knew about it, Cristiano had thought. And because whatever provisions his grandfather had made for Sofia, they had not been in his will, and thus had never been subject to public review or comment.

But there was one person who could not have known about Sofia, or the Cassara family's tacit agreement that she was far, far better for Piero than the angry old woman in the cottage ever could be. And that one person was currently at loose in the villa, clearly digging around in things she shouldn't.

Worse, Cristiano had put her there.

Meaning he had no one to blame for swarming reporters and a breaking new scandal his grandfather would have detested but himself.

He dismissed Massimo, even managing to thank the man. Meanwhile his jaw actually ached as he clenched it, so tight it was a miracle his teeth didn't shatter.

"I have told them to disperse," Massimo said as he walked out of Cristiano's office. "If they do not, I will contact the police."

Cristiano nodded, but there was no getting around what he needed to do, no matter how little he wanted to do it. He had done his best to carry on as usual, pretending there was no woman off in Tuscany and certainly no pregnancy to contend with. Because he had no earthly idea how to handle either one.

And he was not a man who usually suffered from uncertainty.

But he certainly couldn't have Julienne stirring up trouble and breathing life into old scandals that should have stayed buried with his grandfather.

He would have to go to her.

"I will have to go her," he said aloud, as if thinking it wasn't enough. "Damn her."

By the time the helicopter landed near the villa, his temper hadn't cooled a bit. If anything, being back in these rolling fields spiked with cypress trees with the scent of rosemary in the air only made it worse.

Cristiano had been raised mostly in Milan. His father had preferred the city, with its infinite bad choices spread out for him to choose between at his leisure, and he had been deeply scornful of the countryside where he'd been raised. Cristiano had always preferred it here, though he'd known better than to state a preference for anything. He associated the rolling fields and undulating hills so strongly with his grandfather that even now he expected to see the old man waiting for him. His seasons here at the villa were the only times in his life he'd ever really felt *right*.

You should not have brought her here, you fool, he told himself sharply as he made his way toward the sprawling main house his grandfather had restored and rebuilt over the years, so it felt appropriately storied and historic even though every detail had been modernized.

He braced himself as he walked inside, not sure what he expected. The statuary to be upended and left in chunks, perhaps. As if she'd pillaged the place in the week or so since he'd sent her here.

But everything was as he'd left it. And as he liked to leave it in the state his grandfather would recognize if he walked in the door this very evening, Cristiano didn't know how to feel about the fact that Julienne had done the same. Somehow that didn't seem to match a woman who would ring up the tabloids in the next breath.

He wandered through the rooms that looked precisely as they always had, with the same priceless art on the walls and the same furniture that managed to be both sophisticated and comfortable at once. A hallmark of the villa, and in many ways, how he recalled his grandfather, too.

Cristiano wandered across the grand atrium in the center of the building. It was open to the deep blue Tuscany sky above, bursting with flowers, trees and the small pool he knew was stocked with plump, lazy fish.

On the other side, he did not find Julienne in the bedroom suite that had been set aside for her. Or any of the other suites in that wing of the house. And he could admit that he was beginning to feel the faintest sense of unease as he retraced his steps, looking in the various salons and studies and reception rooms, many of which had stood empty since his grandfather's death.

And that was where he found her.

He stopped in the door of the library, watching the light stream in from the great domed skylight above, carefully directed into the center of the space and the table that stood there. And not toward the floor to ceiling shelves that lined the walls. Julienne sat at the table, looking perfectly at her ease. Papers, books, his grandfather's collection of personal letters and a pad she was using to jot down notes were spread across the surface of the center table as if she'd made it her office.

He wanted to charge in and sweep the whole mess of it to the floor, but he couldn't seem to move. Because she was more beautiful than he remembered.

And God help him, but it caught at him. She caught at him and he had no earthly idea how to stop her.

Cristiano could no longer remember, now, how

he'd managed to keep himself from noticing her all these many years. When she'd been nothing to him but another employee, if more ambitious and dependable than most. How had he turned this greed in him off? And why couldn't he do it again?

Her hair was not up in its normal twist today. It swirled down around her shoulders, gleaming gold in the sunlight. She had a faint frown of concentration between her brows, which he wanted to smooth with his fingers. And she tugged her lower lip between her teeth as she scribbled something on the pad before her.

And everything inside him was fire and fury, regret, and that other thing he couldn't quite name. That ache that he couldn't define and was doing his level best to ignore.

He didn't know when she became aware of him. But he knew when she did, even though she didn't react at first. She finished writing whatever she was scribbling on her pad, set her pen down with what struck him as unnecessary precision and only then lifted her gaze to his.

"You've sicced the press on me?" he demanded, his voice not much more than a growl, because that was better than analyzing the *punch* of her gaze. The way it made him want to rock back on his heels. Though he did not. "Do I need to confiscate your mobile, Julienne?"

"You can do that." Her voice was as cool and

mild as her expression. Cristiano believed neither, not when he could still feel that punch. "But then you would have a much bigger problem."

"I find that difficult to believe."

"You've chosen not to deal with me," she said, her eyes dark. "And lucky for you, I am accustomed to taking your orders. But you will find my sister more difficult to control."

"Is that it?" He didn't quite laugh, but he felt... bigger, suddenly. More in control of this mess he'd made. "Your little sister is the threat? Your big gun?"

Julienne smiled. "A key difference between Fleurette and me, among many others, is that she never liked you all that much to begin with."

And Cristiano didn't understand the pull he felt to this woman. He hadn't understood it that night in Monaco. He certainly hadn't understood it in the six long months that had followed. Today, when by rights he should despise her for discussing his family's business with reporters, he found himself leaning against the doorjamb instead. Almost lazily, when he was never lazy.

Almost as if this was some game they played.

"Impossible," he heard himself say, icily sardonic. "My charm is legendary."

"You are a distinctly charmless man," she replied. And there was no reason why Cristiano— who had never given a moment's thought to whether or not he was considered charming by anyone—should feel a sense of outrage at her offhanded, matter-of-fact tone. "You are known chiefly for your intensity, as I think you are well aware. And now, it seems, your upsetting criminal behavior."

Cristiano considered her, feeling as distinctly charmless as she'd called him. "I wonder that you did not call the police rather than the press, if your upset is so great."

She smiled again, but it was a different sort of smile. Far more of a weapon than the politely cool one he'd seen in the office.

"I realize this is not sitting well with you, Cristiano, but you are the father of this baby." Julienne rose then, clearly pointing her belly in his direction. In case he might have forgotten. "And it is not exactly ideal to have the father of my baby locked up forever in prison, as you surely would be if I called the police and explained to them that you're keeping me here against my will."

"You could walk to Florence, *cara*. It is not so many kilometers from here."

"It is, in fact, many hundreds of kilometers to Florence. I checked, and when the maps on my mobile failed, I asked one of your guards."

Cristiano wanted to hurl something back at her, but he was struck by all that light cascading down from above, bathing her in it. She *glowed*. There was no other word to describe it. He tried to tell himself it was a trick of the light, but somehow, he knew perfectly well it was not. It was her.

Julienne was…blooming.

Like the flowers outside in the atrium, she reminded him of spring. Bright and sweet and glowing, like the Roman goddesses who had once been worshiped on this same plot of earth.

"You want my attention, is that it?" he asked, forcing himself to stop thinking about goddesses and *glowing*. "Is that why you sent me your message in the form of a pack of reporters?"

He could hear the danger in his own voice. He thought she heard it too, because she did that thing with her chin. That defiant tilt, as if, left to her own devices, she might fight him.

"It's the baby that needs your attention, Cristiano."

And he had to grit his teeth against that word. *Baby.* Against all the things that happened in him when he thought of it.

Because he knew better. He knew what he was.

"Neither you nor the child will want for anything." His lips thinned. "What more can you require of me than that?"

"Explain to me how this is going to go," she said, in the brisk manner he recognized too well from her days as one of his vice presidents. His favorite vice president, he could admit, now she'd vacated her post. "I will have the baby here, presumably? And I do not doubt that you will see to it that the finest medical team in Europe is on hand. After he is born, I'm sure you will produce nannies. Tutors. Do you anticipate that he will simply live here forever? That he and I will shuffle around the Tuscan hills until we are interred beneath the soil ourselves?"

His teeth ached. Again. "There's no need to be dramatic."

"My mistake. Because there is no inherent drama whatsoever in imprisoning the mother of your child against her will."

"Neither you nor the child will want for anything," he gritted out again, repeating himself.

"The child will want a father," she threw back at him. "And I—"

But she stopped herself. And he found himself roaming closer, not sure what it was that compelled him. That glow of hers, maybe, now mixed with the heat of her temper.

Cristiano had never seen anything so bright.

And he could not tell if he wanted to lock her away or put his hands on her instead. He could not tell which one hurt, which tempted him or how on earth he could possibly handle this. Her.

The baby.

"Finish your sentence," he dared her. "What is it *you* want, Julienne?"

"I have known you for a long time, Cristiano. A very long time. I have seen the best of you first-hand. I have also seen you on one of your cold rampages, striking terror into whole divisions with a single stare."

"And yet you do not know me at all," he retorted.

"I know enough. You have your rules, don't you? You like to be alone. No friends, no family, only work. You like a woman, but only for a night."

"In this, I think you'll find, I am no different than any other man."

"But you're not a playboy, forever in search of flesh and sin," she said, and there was a different kind of light in her dark eyes. He could feel the echo of it inside him. "You're afraid."

CHAPTER SEVEN

IF SHE'D THROWN a lit match at him, she doubted Cristiano would look more thunderstruck.

But that was good, she assured herself as that thunderstruck expression tipped over into something significantly more forbidding. He might not want to know how she felt, but she was compelled to tell him anyway, for her sins.

There had to be something deeply wrong with her that this man—her *captor*, lest she forgot— could stride in here with a look on his face that suggested she was already trying his patience, and she should want nothing more than to go to him. To put her hands on him. To press her mouth to his and feel the kick of that race through her all over again.

"Call the police," Fleurette had snapped at her, the first day. And every day since. "Or I will."

"I can't call the police," Julienne replied every time. Today she'd added, "think of the baby, please, Fleurette. Does he need to come into the world to find his father in jail?"

But her sister knew her too well, and had responded to that pious tone with a snort.

"Maybe you should think of the baby," she'd shot right back. "With your head, Julienne. Instead of whatever it is you're thinking with these days."

Julienne did not wish to examine what part of her person she might have been using lately, thank you. What mattered was that there would be no police. Paparazzi, perhaps, thanks to the wealth of personal letters Cristiano's grandfather had kept in this library. Passionate letters, both the ones he'd received and copies of those he'd sent, which meant Julienne had the full picture of his extramarital affair—a relationship filled with longing and complaint, years of yearning and plans for more. Always more.

And privately, she might have felt somewhat ashamed about sharing those sentiments with the world by calling some of the contacts she'd made in her time at Cassara Chocolates, then letting them run with what she'd dug up. Then again, who wasn't fascinated with stories of marital infidelity, long-term mistresses paraded around in plain view, and the truth about great men who had been very nearly canonized after their deaths?

Besides, she told herself now as Cristiano scowled at her, what else was she supposed to do?

She was a kidnap victim. A kidnap victim held in glorious luxury, it was true, but all the lovely trappings in the world couldn't change the fact she couldn't leave.

Oh, said a voice inside her that sounded far too much like her sister, *do you* want *to leave? Because that certainly isn't clear.*

That landed like a punch. Because Julienne knew, now, that anything she might have told herself about her motivations was a lie. She'd known that the moment she'd looked up and seen him there, smoldering and furious and still with that darkness all over his face.

As if she had not simply surprised him with this baby. As if she'd broken him instead. A notion that made her want to reach out and make it better, somehow, with her hands.

Fleurette would be appalled, she knew. But then, Fleurette was often and easily appalled. It was part of her charm.

"I must have misheard you, Julienne," Cristiano said after what felt like a long, long while, in a conversational tone she in no way believed. Not when she could see that simmering fury in his dark gaze. "It sounded as if you called me a coward."

"It's a choice you have to make," she threw back at him, head high, as if he didn't get to her at all. Because he shouldn't have gotten to her. "You can be a father or you can be afraid. So far, it appears you've chosen the latter."

Because surely they could both figure out how to be better parents than the ones they'd had. She had to believe that was possible.

Cristiano's glower took on a new weight, but she refused to be cowed. And as he prowled toward her, she reminded herself that he hadn't exactly become less dangerous in the week he'd left her here.

What was wrong with her that something in her thrilled to that?

And worse, there was that melting between her legs. As if her body had already made its choices and would happily, exultantly, make them all over again.

"You are not the only person I met in that bar ten years ago," he told her when he reached the table.

She felt a jolt at that, an awful kick. Was he trying to say…? But she couldn't even complete that question in her own head.

"I was there in the first place because I knew my father was there that night," he continued, sounding even darker than before. "He loved Monte Carlo. The excess soothed him. And when I found him, he was blind drunk, as ever. But in his blindness he retained a certain, vicious clarity. Particularly when it came to me."

"*In vino veritas* is a lie," Julienne said quietly,

something she knew all too well. And she refused to acknowledge the sense of deep relief she felt that he was not telling her a story of how he'd had some other woman in that place she now thought of as theirs—the good and bad of it alike. "You must have learned the truth of this years ago."

Cristiano's mouth did something stark and bitter. "My father was not pleased to see me, which was the typical state of affairs between us."

That bitter curve to his mouth only deepened, leaving brackets in his hard face. And Julienne wished, suddenly, that he had not started to tell her this tale. She had a terrible feeling about where he was going with it.

But she couldn't seem to speak when she needed to most.

Cristiano kept going, one hand on the table between them. "We had a fundamental disagreement, my father and I. He believed that it was his right to behave as he wished, without a single thought for any other living human being. In particular, my mother, who he took great pleasure in bullying. And I believed that if he wanted to careen about from one bottle to the next, then communicate with his fists, he should remove himself entirely from the rest of polite society. These were incompatible positions, obviously."

And there was something about the way he was looking at her, that bittersweet gaze of his direct.

Intense. Daring her to…argue? Deny him the opportunity to tell this story? She couldn't tell. But whatever he was daring her to do, it made her pulse pick up. Her heart began to kick through her, slow and hard and insistent.

"I had long ago outgrown any need to rail at my father in the hope that he would become a different man before my eyes. Those are trials of adolescence and I had long ago become inured to his opinions of me. They mattered less and less in the course of my actual life and work. Left to my own devices, I rarely saw him."

"Except that night," Julienne managed to croak out, though her throat felt almost too tight to bear.

"That night it was necessary for me to seek him out," Cristiano agreed, the banked fury in that dark gaze of his making her neck prickle. "It was not a task I relished, though if I am honest, there was a part of me that wanted it, too. My grandfather was concerned about the future of the company he had spent his life building. He was as disgusted with my father as I was was—more, probably. And after many years spent waiting and hoping that my father might straighten himself out and rejoin the family and the company as a contributing member, my grandfather had made a final decision. He'd gone ahead and cut my father off entirely. And had written him out of his will to boot."

Julienne wanted to reach for him, but knew that

Cristiano would never allow it. He stood too stiffly. His eyes were too dark. She braced her hands on the swell of her belly, and tried to focus on the story he was telling. And not how she longed to soothe a man who didn't want to feel better. Who would actively avoid it if possible, in fact.

"Why were you the messenger?" she asked quietly instead, a sense of injustice welling up in her on his behalf. "Shouldn't this have been something your grandfather told your father himself? It was his will."

"My father and I did not see each other much, but my father and my grandfather had not spoken in years," Cristiano said with a certain briskness that told Julienne a great many things about his family without him having to elaborate. And it occurred to her to wonder why she had always assumed that someone with his money must necessarily have no problems. Why she'd imagined that the money itself would protect him, when, of course, complicated people kept right on complicating things no matter their tax bracket. "It fell to me to deliver the news to him, if I chose."

"If you chose?"

"I didn't have to tell him that night. I could have waited for the inevitable explosion when he discovered his funding had disappeared, and for good. I might have, were it not for my mother."

Julienne blinked. "She wasn't still with him. Was she?"

"My mother believed deeply in the sanctity of marriage," Cristiano replied, his voice as hard as it was cold. As if he was turning to ice before her eyes. "Or perhaps it was more that she felt she had made her bed and was required to lie in it ever after. I can't say. I understood her very little, if I'm honest."

Julienne shook her head. "But surely she wasn't required to stay if your father was cruel to her."

"There is no 'get out of jail' card for a bad marriage," Cristiano said, a hard amusement in his voice that in no way made it to his eyes. "Not for my mother. She was raised to endure. This story you have dug up about my grandfather and Sofia Tomasi—I used to tell my mother that she should use it as her example. That it was possible to have something better. Different, anyway, even if she did choose to remain married. But she was horrified at the very idea."

"So she stayed."

"She endured." Cristiano blew out a breath. "I admired my grandfather deeply. In many ways, he is the only hero I have ever known. But when he cut off my father, I knew that he was condemning my mother to more abuse. It was the only time we fought."

Julienne searched his face, but there was only

granite. "Did you think that if you spoke to your father he'd be nicer to your mother? I would have been afraid that it would make him go in the opposite direction."

"I did not beg a man like Giacomo Cassara to treat his wife better." Cristiano's eyes gleamed with that cold near amusement that made Julienne shiver. "I wanted him to know first that despite his best efforts, his inheritance was mine. And second, that I didn't care what he did with himself, but I would be watching over my mother. And prepared to take matters into my own hands if any harm befell her."

Julienne's mind spun. She tried to remember the bits and pieces of Cassara family history that had trickled down to her over the years. This rumor, that rumor. She knew his mother was no longer alive, of course. But did that mean…?

"My father proceeded to tell me that he thought about drowning me when I was a child. Repeatedly. Among other, less savory parental notions." Cristiano paused, his mouth in a flat, hard line. "And then he staggered out of the bar. He collected my mother where, unbeknownst to me, she was waiting for him in a rented flat, and told the valet that he was driving them back to Milan. Meanwhile, I looked up from a dark contemplation of the only example of fatherhood I knew personally…to find you there. Determined to sell yourself."

"Whatever your father said to you is a reflection of him, not you. You must know that."

"Spare me the pop psychology, please." His dark eyes glittered, remote and icily furious at once. "You and I can sit here and discuss at length the ways in which my father was a pathetic example of a man. But that does not change the fact there is something wrong with me. With this blood in my veins."

She opened her mouth to argue, but a frigid glare stopped her.

"I always think of my grandfather as a good man, but as you have uncovered, there are reasons to think otherwise. If you traipsed across the length of this property and found my grandmother, she would tell you that the Cassaras are nothing but monsters. Devils sent to this earth to plague the decent."

"In fairness, it seems your grandfather was fairly unrepentant about the fact he was cheating on her." Julienne gestured at the table and the collection of letters. "He even brags about it."

"There was only one good Cassara, and he died a long time ago," Cristiano said. Firmly. "I never had any plans for there to be another."

"Cristiano…"

"But there is more to the story." And she was

too well trained to obey that commanding voice of his. She'd been doing it for years. She fell silent without even meaning to do so while he kept telling her this same story that bookended hers. "While I was busy making arrangements for you and your sister and having you transported out of the country, my father was driving to Milan. But he never made it."

The memory, foggy before, snapped back into place. There had been a car accident. She remembered the whispers she'd heard in the office about his past. And even more vaguely, the research she'd done on his family when he'd first installed them in the house in Milan.

But she didn't want him to say it. Not here. She wanted to leap across the sun-drenched library table and throw her hands over his mouth to keep his words in.

As if that could make it any better for him.

The baby kicked then. Hard. Sharing her distress, maybe, And for a moment she didn't have to wonder why she couldn't breathe.

"They say he lost control of the car in the Montferrat hills. But I know better. He was already drunk, and I had agitated him. And I'm not going to stand here and pretend to you that the loss of a man like my father keeps me up at night. It doesn't. It's my mother I can't let go." Cristiano's hard gaze bored into her. "He killed my mother, and it was my fault, and I have to live with that."

"Cristiano—"

"And then I have to ask myself, what kind of man does not care that he sent his own father to his death?"

"It wasn't your fault," Julienne said fiercely. She stepped out from behind the table and moved toward him, even though it was foolish. She couldn't seem to help herself. "You weren't the one who'd had too much to drink. You weren't driving the car."

"I knew what he was and I knew what might happen if he went off half-cocked. This is what I'm talking about, Julienne." And she could see something besides that glacial cold in his dark eyes as she came closer. The torture. The pain. Her stomach twisted—*for* him. "I killed my mother as surely as if I was behind the wheel. And I let my father kill the both of them, because some part of me cared that little about where he would go and what he would do once he left that bar. Because the truth is, there is nothing good in me. I play a good game, but scratch the surface, and I'm nothing but another Cassara monster. A breaker of vows. A bully. A son who took great pleasure in taunting his father into staggering off and getting behind the wheel. One way or another, that makes me a killer."

Julienne felt like crying. Or possibly already was. Her eyes were glassy and the library was becoming blurred at the edges.

But in the center of everything was Cristiano.

"None of that is true," she managed to say.

And then she closed the last bit of distance between them and slid her hands on his chest.

He jolted as if she'd shocked him. His hands moved to capture hers, and she thought he would push her away, but he didn't.

And for a very long moment, they stood there, frozen.

"You are nothing like your father," she told him with all the ferocity she could muster. "I knew your grandfather too, don't forget, and the difference between you and him is that you don't make vows unless you know you can keep them. Forever. There are a thousand things that can make an innocent child grow into a man like your father, but none of them are in your blood, Cristiano. Not one of them."

And before he could argue any further, she thrust herself up on her tiptoes, somehow balancing the weight of her belly, and pressed a kiss to his mouth.

She hadn't meant to do that.

Or maybe she had, because Lord knew, every night she tried to sleep in this villa—this gorgeous prison—and her head was full of nothing but him.

Images of the things they'd done. Of the things they might yet do. She woke up in the dark, her body one great throbbing pulse of need, and he was never there.

But Cristiano was here now. And he was hurting.

And somehow a kiss seemed to be the answer to everything. A give and a take. A soothing and a sharing, for both of them.

So she angled her head and took it deeper.

Just the way he'd taught her.

She felt him shake. It was as if he was melting, there while she touched him, and she knew that if he was in control of himself the way he normally was, he would never have allowed it. He would certainly never have let her *see* it.

She had the sense of glaciers melting, ice floes cracking.

Until slowly, almost reluctantly, he kissed her back.

And she forgot, for a moment, that he had spirited her off to this place. She forgot the baby. The great belly that was now pressed between them.

Cristiano kissed her and she forgot her own name.

She heard a faint noise, low and greedy, and only belatedly realized that it was her. That it was coming from her own throat.

And when he tore his mouth from hers, he looked hunted. *Haunted,* something in her supplied.

With perhaps more satisfaction than necessary.

"It is already too much," he said, dark and low. "It is already gone too far."

"I don't know what that means." But she understood well enough when he stepped away, backing away from her as if she'd *done something* to him. "Are you disgusted by my pregnancy?" Her voice was much too brittle, but she did nothing to stop it. She couldn't. "Is that what this is?"

"You *glow*," he bit out, as if the words erupted from within. "If it is possible, you're more beautiful now than you were before, damn you. And I think you know it."

That was meant to be an indictment, clearly. He threw it at her, then wheeled around, and stalked away.

And Julienne should no doubt have taken herself off for another good cry.

But instead, she found herself standing there where Cristiano had left her, her mouth still tingling from the taste of him, and a smile she couldn't quite control on her face.

CHAPTER EIGHT

THE WOMAN WAS a demon.

There was no other explanation for that kiss. The way he'd responded and worse, what he'd said to her as he walked away. This was precisely what he'd wanted to avoid. It was why he'd stashed her away in Tuscany in the first place.

Did you really think she wouldn't cause problems for you? a harsh voice inside him asked. *If you wanted to keep her out of trouble, you should have made sure she couldn't contact the outside world. A prison isn't much of a prison when a person has full access to her media contacts, is it?*

Cristiano meant to return to Milan. He needed to keep away from this woman who had unaccountably haunted him long before she'd turned up pregnant. But halfway to the helicopter, he thought better of it. Leaving Julienne to her own devices helped no one, least of all him. Especially not when he was stalked by the reporters she'd sent after the family secrets.

Unapologetically.

That was what he told himself, in any case, as he sent for his things and then set up his usual remote office in the villa.

His intention—had anyone asked, which no one would dare—was simply to monitor the situation here. To repress any further attempts to stir up trouble.

Even if he still didn't know why he'd shared the details of that night in Monaco with her, when he'd never talked about that night with anyone. Much less the guilt and shame he carried with him even now.

And once in the villa, he expected her to show that relentless streak he'd so admired when she'd worked for him. He expected interrogations over his morning cappuccino, demands for further discussions at the end of his work day, or appearances in the middle of conference calls that would cause him difficulties with his colleagues when so many of them knew her.

But Julienne did none of these things.

She appeared at dinner that first night looking fresh and easy, seeming to shine even brighter than before. The smile she aimed his way was sunny, which had the direct result of making him glower.

"The staff tell me that you have insisted on a

solitary dinner service every night," he said, sitting in his usual spot at the head of the grand table, the centerpiece of the formal dining room. "Right here at this table."

She beamed at him, sitting directly to his right. "There have to be some perks to finding oneself marooned in Tuscany. I decided I might as well make use of your fine staff and your truly excellent cook."

And when Cristiano could seem to do nothing at all but stare darkly at her, she smiled again, even more sunnily. Then she turned her attention to her antipasti.

He resolved to use this experience—sharing the villa with her, against his will—as an opportunity for some immersion therapy. He did not wish to be haunted, thank you. He wanted her out of his head, his unfortunate dreams, his life. Cristiano felt certain that familiarity must breed its usual contempt, and that in short order this *thing* that ate away at him would disappear completely.

Once it did, he could approach the rest of this rationally. Carefully.

But everywhere he went, she seemed to be there. Even if she was not physically in the room, there was some reminder of her. Her scent on the breeze, or the sound of her laughter from across the atrium.

More than that, the woman he associated so

strongly with a particular corporate sleekness and style of dress preferred to go about...naked.

Well. Not precisely *naked*.

But as the weather got warmer, Julienne could often be found out at the swimming pool, set slightly down the hill from the house, sunning herself.

Wearing absolutely nothing but a bikini.

And he had not lied to her that day in the library. He found her new, impossibly lush body astonishingly beautiful. Almost too beautiful to bear.

He might not want to think of his impending fatherhood. He actively avoided it, in fact. But it was impossible not to look at Julienne and think of fertility. Of spring and sunshine, colorful new flowers and the fresh green of new growth.

She was bright and round and ripe, and every moment he did not have his hands on her was a torment.

Cristiano found himself in his own hell. Here at the villa, where he had always come for sanity. For an escape from the tumultuous life his parents led. One week led into the next, a riot of longing and fury, Julienne's knowing smiles, and those dinners that required more self-control than they should have.

Familiarity with Julienne bred nothing like contempt. On the contrary, it ignited nothing short of an obsession.

But he knew addicts too well. And he knew that succumbing to the itch was always worse, in the long run. Always. Far better to white knuckle his way through this without sampling her again.

Sooner or later, this vice grip she had on him would fade. He was sure of it.

One night at dinner, she looked up from the gazpacho that had been served as their first course and announced that the doctor would be coming the following morning.

"It was so thoughtful of you to set up an obstetrician's office of sorts in one of the studies," she said, in that tone of hers he spent far too much time analyzing. Was she mocking him? Was that a hint of a sardonic slap? Or had he gone utterly mad and was now *parsing* her tone? "If you come to the appointment tomorrow, you'll be able to see—"

"'Come'?" Cristiano stared at her from across the table, the icy distance he preferred to keep between them crumbling into so much ash. "Why would I attend your doctor's appointment?"

And for the first time since he'd come here, that sunny, breezy demeanor of hers cracked.

First, that smile tumbled from her face. Her gaze darkened. She put her fork down and took a breath, as if he was trying her patience. And more—messing with her head the way she was doing with his.

Funny how that seemed a hollow victory.

"What game are you playing, Cristiano?" she demanded, an undercurrent in her voice that made his chest tight. "Why would you be here, however reluctantly, if you didn't want some part in your son's life?"

Cristiano stared back at her as if he was made entirely from stone. It would be easier if he was, he knew. "I'm here to encourage you not to continue to seed the voracious Italian press with scandalous stories about my grandfather," he told her, crisply, as if he couldn't see the dark thing between them. Not even now it was all over her lovely face. "And if I cannot encourage you to stop, to prevent you from doing it all the same."

Julienne sat back in her seat, her belly taking up most of the room between them. Or so it seemed to him, because that gloriously round belly was all he could see.

She studied him for far too long. With a considering sort of look in her clever eyes that made him feel far too exposed. "Let me guess. This is your fear talking. Again."

He didn't like that. "I am who I am. Who I have always been in all the years you have known me. It is hardly my fault if you cannot accept this now that you are with child." He shrugged. "Perhaps this is an example of the pregnancy hormones I have heard so much about."

There was hot color on her cheeks, then, and

something perilously close to disappointment in her eyes. When, if he was honest with himself, it had been his intention to prick her temper.

Not disappoint her.

He had already disappointed the first woman who had ever meant something to him. He couldn't bear the idea that he was doing it again.

"People choose who they are," Julienne told him, her voice much too quiet. Not shrill, not furious. Just that quiet directness that scraped at him, leaving deep grooves inside her. "Every day, you choose. It's not destiny that makes a man, or his bloodline. It's how he behaves."

"You have no idea what you're talking about."

"You forget how you met me," she shot back.

Cristiano had not forgotten. And now, because of what had happened ten years later, all his memories of her were infused with an eroticism the reality had not possessed. Like all those years in offices around the world when he somehow hadn't fully looked at her. He remembered them like torture now. And when he thought of Monte Carlo now, she was this version of Julienne both times— not the terrified sixteen-year-old she'd been then.

You are sick, he accused himself. *Do you need any further proof?*

But then, he had despaired of himself for the whole of the last decade.

"You never asked either one of us too much

about where we came from," Julienne said now, still sitting back in her chair and frowning at him. "Which was a mercy, as neither Fleurette nor I ever wanted to speak of it. You told me that first night that you assumed that if selling my body was my only option, my other options must be wretched indeed."

"You have mentioned your mother before," he said darkly. He didn't wish to have this conversation. Or any conversation. He wanted to remain in merry ignorance forever, if that would keep this woman at arm's length. If that was what he wanted. Which, he assured himself forcefully then, he did. Of course he did. "I understand that your childhood was unpleasant."

If she heard his repressive tones, she ignored it.

"In my village, they called my mother a 'party girl,'" Julienne told him. "A lovely euphemism, is it not? When what she was, always, was an addict. She had me when she was seventeen. Sometimes she liked to claim that I ruined her life, but even as a child, I knew that wasn't true. She was the one who ruined her life, over and over again."

"I don't see what the story has to do with our situation," Cristiano said gruffly.

Because the last thing he needed was to have more reasons to *feel things* where this woman was concerned.

"It's hard for me to look back and figure out

what I knew then and what I know now, thanks to the passing of so many years." Julienne sighed. "But my mother would do anything for a good time. At a certain point they began to tease me about it in school. Everyone knew who the easiest woman in the village was, and how they could get their hands on her. So you see, when I decided to sell myself, I knew what to do. I thought I would try to differentiate myself from my poor mother by charging more than a pack of cigarettes or a ride home."

His jaw was so tight he worried it might shatter. "I do not see the purpose of wandering off down memory lane, Julienne."

But she didn't relent. "Men began to look at me early. Too early. There were leers, suggestive comments. One of my mother's friends told me that the Boucher women had a certain look. That anyone could tell they were made to be whores. And yes, he said *women*. He wanted to be sure to include Fleurette, who could not have been more than eight at the time. It was as if we had price tags around our necks, and a clock counting down. All the men in that village were waiting for was the opportunity."

That chin of hers rose, defiant and something more.

And there was a howl in him that Cristiano doubted would ever fade.

Julienne's smile was brittle. "On the day I decided to leave that town forever, I had been propositioned no less than three times. It was just an ordinary day. And I knew, you see, that it was only a matter of time before I surrendered to my fate. There was nowhere to go on that cursed hill. No one would hire one of the Boucher women to do an honest job. Who would have a whore like that behind the counter? Or even sweeping a floor where decent people might go?"

"Why are you telling me this?" Cristiano demanded, convinced there was ground glass in his mouth as he spoke. "Is it your intention that I find this village and burn it to the ground?"

He would do it personally. And with pleasure.

"You are a Cassara," she threw at him, her voice fierce, then. "The blood you are so ashamed to have in your veins makes you a billionaire twice over. You can buy anything you wish. You were never trapped in a forgotten hill town, doomed to be a whore. And yes, I was lucky enough to stumble upon a benefactor at the least likely moment. But I didn't lounge about, bemoaning my good luck. I claimed it. Don't you see? I worked night and day to be worthy of my rescue."

Cristiano didn't know when he had stopped pretending to pick at his dinner. Or when they'd faced off, there at the corner of the great table in the dining room, staring each other down as if at any moment one of them might throw a punch.

What was wrong with him that he almost thought it would be a relief?

"I know you cannot be suggesting that I am... lazy, is it?"

"Not lazy, perhaps. But you certainly do work at your self-pity the way others work for a paycheck."

He growled. "Be very, very careful, *cara*."

"Or what?" Julienne asked wildly, and laughed in a way he could not say he enjoyed at all. "Let me guess. You will imprison me on a remote property and leave me to live out my days in forced solitude. That will show me."

"Here is one thing you apparently did not learn in your vicious little hill town." He leaned closer to her, which was a mistake. "Things can always get worse. They often do."

Julienne sighed, a great heaving sound, as if plagued. By him, presumably.

"When our son is old enough, will you sit right here this table and tell him these things?" she demanded. When he was used to making the demands in all situations. "Will you make certain to let him know that he's cursed already? As doomed as I was? How will you make sure that he's aware of the Cassara corrosion that already pollutes him?"

Cristiano found he couldn't answer that. He

only stared back at her, something dark and edgy gripping him. Crushing him.

"When he seeks his father for comfort, will you push him down to the ground? Slap him until he cries—or stops crying? That's what your father did to you, didn't he?"

"Stop it," he ordered her, with a stranger's voice.

But her eyes were too bright with an emotion he couldn't identify.

"I know. You'll wait until he really needs you. When he's a man grown but still needs a father figure. You'll get drunk. You'll say appalling things, calculated to slice him into pieces. Then you'll totter out of the bar, hurt yourself, and blame him for it."

She might as well have thrown a bomb at him. Cristiano wished she had.

"That is more than enough," he growled at her. "I believe you've made your point."

But he could see that wild thing was still on her, in her. She stared straight at him, challenge stamped on every inch of her, opened her mouth—

And Cristiano did not want to hear whatever came next.

He pushed back from his chair, hardly aware that he was moving, and then he was looming over her. But that was good, because she sucked in a breath. And did not say whatever shattering thing was next on her list.

A win, as far as he was concerned.

He pulled out her chair so he could lean down over her and brace himself on the arms, holding her there.

And he remembered, with an electric flash of need and longing, that night in Monte Carlo. That alcove he'd found off the lobby.

He could tell from the way her breath changed and her color heightened that she remembered it too.

"You poke and poke and poke," he said, his voice so low he wasn't certain it was anything more than a dark rumble. "You must know that this cannot end well, Julienne."

"That's the point," she threw back at him, defiant to the end, which made him feel…something almost like helpless, in the face of all her beauty and resolve. "It never will end, Cristiano. If all goes according to plan, a father dies before his son. And you have to ask yourself a question, right now. Do you want your son to talk about you the way you talk about your own father? Or do you want something better for both of you?"

"I told you, no more. No more, Julienne."

He didn't raise his voice so much as he leaned into the way he said the words, staining them both with all that intensity inside of him.

Julienne didn't flinch. She didn't so much as bat an eye. He watched her breathe, watched those extra full breasts move, and her belly with it. And it occurred to him that he was most furious with her not because she was wrong.

But because he had the terrible suspicion that she was right.

Cristiano couldn't face it. So he bent down instead, took her defiant chin in his hand, and kissed her.

And he could not have said the things that battled inside him, then. He wouldn't have known where to begin.

The losses he had suffered, one after the next. His enduring shame and guilt, first because there was something about him that had made his own father hate him as a child. And then later, that he had hated his father enough in return to let him stumble out of that bar and toward the certain death he should have anticipated would steal away his mother, too.

He had let it happen. Or he hadn't cared enough to stop it.

His hands were stained with the blood of two deaths that he could have prevented.

If only he had been a different man.

He wanted to forget. He wanted her shine, her light, *that glow* instead.

Cristiano kissed her and he kissed her.

He kissed her for the baby she carried, the son he'd never wanted. He kissed her for the challenges she'd thrown at him, her refusal to quietly disappear the way he'd wanted, and because she still haunted him. Here, now, while he touched her, she haunted him.

Something in him rang, deep and hard, and he had the uncomfortable notion she always would.

And then, somehow, he was sinking down to his knees before her, to worship her properly.

Again.

"Cristiano..." she breathed, but he didn't want her words.

He wanted her passion. He wanted her taste in his mouth and the molten hot clench of her body on his. He *wanted*—and he was done restraining himself.

Julienne liked to dress for dinner, in what he was certain was—like that bikini of hers—a calculated campaign to make him lose his mind. It obviously worked all too well. Tonight's selection was a formfitting, stretchy sort of dress that covered her modestly enough and yet was deeply, spectacularly immodest at the same time because it welded itself to her curves. It emphasized those full, heavy breasts, all but making love to her enormous bump.

Cristiano did the same.

He found her breasts with his hands and teased her nipples in his palms. Slowly, carefully, not sure what kind of sensation she would like now, he moved his hands in circles.

And watched her come apart.

Her head fell back. She let out a moan he was fairly certain he'd last heard when he was deep inside of her, and he felt the spike of it like her mouth along the length of him.

He kept going, playing with one nipple, then the other. He watched in fascination as her cheeks went red, goose bumps rose along her skin, and then, unmistakably, she convulsed.

She bucked in the chair and he moved closer, wedging his body between her legs. Then he hissed out a breath when he felt the molten center of her against his thigh.

"You have said a great deal tonight, *cara*," he told her, murmuring the words into the side of her neck. "But as always, I'm only interested in one word. My name. I think we both know how easily it falls off your tongue."

And then he moved down her body, helping himself to every last voluptuous inch of this new body of hers. Her glorious breasts, that swollen belly. And when he got to her thighs, he pushed the stretchy material of her dress out of his way, then up further, until he bared her to his view. He made short work of the panties she wore, tossing them aside, and then settling down to get a taste of her. Rich, sweet.

Ripe and entirely his.

He hadn't allowed himself to think too closely about all the various things she'd said to him since she'd reappeared in his life, but suddenly, all he could think about was the fact of her innocence that night in Monte Carlo.

Only mine, a dark voice in him intoned. *Only and ever mine.*

He took a deep, lush taste, and kept going until she was squirming against him, panting out his name the way he liked. Only then did he pull away.

He lifted her up, enjoying the extra heft her roundness gave her. He moved her onto the gleaming, polished table, then spread her out beneath the sparkling chandelier that dated back to the time of kings and royal guests at Villa Cassara.

Then, finally, he pulled that dress from her body, and made short work of her bra. And then she was there before him in all her glory. His very own goddess, her eyes glazed with heat and need.

He pulled himself out from his trousers, already huge and ready. And he watched her face change, going hungry.

It was the sexiest thing he'd ever seen.

Cristiano braced himself on the tabletop, moved his hips to hers, and slowly, deliberately, sheathed himself in the molten grasp of her core with a single, relentless thrust.

Julienne shattered at once. Her back arched, offering all her deliciously full curves to him.

But he waited. He gritted his teeth as her pleasure washed over him, through him, and nearly sent him spiraling off into his own.

Once her initial storm passed, he began to move.

He went carefully at first, but when her response was nothing but enthusiastic, he thrust a little harder. A little deeper.

Until the two of them were moving as one, fighting together to get to that same great height that had stalked him since Monaco. That sweet rush that haunted him, night and day.

And she said his name the way he'd told her to. She sang it, over and over, until he could not tell the difference between the melody and the name itself.

Between his name and her and this magic they made between the two of them.

And when it all broke apart, sending them both shattering, he was the one who cried out. He was the one who called her name like a summoning, a reckoning.

Like a new song.

And he didn't know how long they stayed like that, there on that antique table where his grandfather had entertained Europe's finest, in his time.

He didn't care, either. Minutes, hours, years. As long as she was with him, curled around him, a part of him—

But he didn't allow himself to finish that thought.

He pulled himself away from her with more reluctance than was healthy or wise. He tucked himself into his trousers, and then, without thinking it through, lifted her up into his arms.

She dropped her head to his shoulder, and he felt a surge of feeling he couldn't begin to identify wash over him. Something he might have called tender, if he was that kind of man. If there was anything soft inside him.

If there was, it was only hers.

A thought that should have disturbed him, but he shoved it aside.

And he carried her from the grand dining room, through the villa, until he found the master bedroom. Once there, he settled her in his bed.

He did not question himself. He did not analyze what he was doing. He simply did it.

Cristiano busied himself removing his own clothes. He was crawling back into the bed beside her when she opened her eyes again, fixed them on him and smiled.

Light. Heat.

Joy, even.

And he didn't know what to do with the things in him that rose to meet that smile. Something like wonder, God help him. And a strange tenderness that would likely appall him, come morning.

But it was still night. And more than anything

else, there was still that driving greed that made him reach for her all over again.

"Am I allowed to talk yet?" she asked softly, her smile firming into a solemn line, though her eyes still laughed at him, toffee-colored and sweet.

"Of course," he said, rolling her into him. "You have one word, as always. Use it well."

Cristiano did not need words. He didn't know the right ones—or worse, he did, but could not bring himself to say them. Because he had always known who he was. He had always known that he did not have the same capacities in him that others did, or his own father would not have despised him. And he, in turn, would not have let him leave that bar in Monaco while so impaired.

Love was for other people. Tenderness was a dream.

He had always prided himself on his directness instead.

So he used his mouth on her in other ways, his hands and the hardest part of him too, while she sang that song of hers.

That beautiful song that was in him now. The song he knew he would never escape, as long as he lived.

He used what he had and he told her all those things he could never say out loud, never in words. He told her over and over again, until dawn.

When the sun rose over the Tuscan hills and Cristiano was still himself.

Always and ever himself, and destined therefore to remain alone.

CHAPTER NINE

CRISTIANO WAS NOT in the bed when she woke.

"That's quite all right," Julienne muttered to herself, running her hand over her belly to say her usual hello to the baby. "It would be far more surprising if he was here, really."

And the baby was still sleeping, or unwilling to give her even a little kick, so she heaved herself up and over to the side of the bed. After hesitating a moment, she stole a silk robe from his vast dressing room, then padded her way down the hall to her own suite.

Where, if she wanted to have an emotion or two in her shower or while fixing her hair, that was no one's business but hers.

She expected to see him at breakfast out on one of the patios these warm, bright mornings, while Tuscany outdid itself with its spring splendor in all directions. But when she made it to the patio in question, Cristiano was nowhere to be found.

That's just as well, too, she told herself stoutly.

Maybe if she kept telling herself that she'd believe it.

The gardeners had outdone themselves with the rose bushes, and it was strange how little she fancied cut roses, as ubiquitous as they were. And yet here, where they grew exultantly around the villa, seemingly on the verge of going wild at any moment, she couldn't seem to get enough of them.

And there was a lesson there, likely having to do with the thorns.

But then, all things involving the Cassara family were bad for her in one way or another. And here she still was. With the next Cassara currently inside her, pressing hard on her solar plexus when he was in a mood.

And she knew she was a goner when the image of a tiny little Cassara deliberately kicking at her made her laugh.

"I'll be mounting a rescue operation," Fleurette announced later that morning, her voice tense over the phone. "I don't think I've ever gone this long without seeing you. It's not okay. You know that, I hope. *None of this is okay.* If I have to storm Tuscany to make it clear to that man, I will."

Julienne laughed. She had spent some more time with Piero Cassara's letters after breakfast, but somehow hadn't been able to bring herself to make any further calls to her contacts. Fleurette's number flashing on her phone had been a relief—because anything was better than facing her own weaknesses, surely. Even sharp conversations with her sister.

"One does not storm Tuscany, Fleurette," she said, still laughing. "One flies into Florence, becomes operatic at the sight of the Arno, and loses oneself for days between the Ponte Vecchio and Neptune's marble penis."

"I've waited in line for the Uffizi, thank you, and it wasn't worth it. This isn't a joke that you can tell about penises on Florentine statues, Julienne. We're talking about Cristiano Cassara locking you away forever. I'm not going to let him do that. And while we're on the topic, he's certainly not barring me from my nephew's birth, either. I don't care what he did for us ten years ago."

"Fleurette." Julienne kept her voice as mild as possible, because she knew her sister well. And she knew where Fleurette's vehemence came from. "You know I love you. And I know that there are very good reasons that you want to rescue me this time. But I don't need rescuing. I'm not Maman."

"Are you sure about that?" Her sister asked, her voice thick with those memories she usually pretended not to have. "Because an addict is an addict as far as I can see."

And then rang off before Julienne could counter, which might have been childish, but was also effective.

Maybe too effective, because she left Julienne stewing.

So much, in fact, that Julienne was late to her own doctor's appointment, even if it was conveniently located right there in the villa. She'd been too busy thinking about addictions. About all the different ways a person could give herself over to something more powerful than she was, particularly when it was bad for her.

She'd seen what it had done to Annette. But she'd never given any thought to the fact that before her mother's many crushes, there was first the exultation.

And she wasn't sure how she felt about the fact that she understood that now.

"I'm so sorry," she said as she walked into the study that had been made into a remarkably well-furnished doctor's office, just for her. "I didn't mean to keep you waiting."

The doctor gave her a slight bow, which struck her as strange. *He thinks you're the new lady of the manor,* a voice inside piped up, *and now that Cristiano is here, he thinks he needs to treat you with more respect.*

Julienne really should have made it clear that she and Cristiano weren't…anything. Not really, or she wouldn't be here alone, would she? But she was late this morning. And slightly off balance for any number of reasons, from last night to her sister to her own inability to be as ruthless as she knew she should have been, so she…said nothing. The doctor could think what he liked.

She answered the usual questions, then got up on the exam table and waited while he and his nurse hooked her up to all the state-of-the-art machines Cristiano's people had installed in here.

Because Cristiano might claim he wanted nothing to do with his baby, but he still made sure that both Julienne and that baby were well cared for. No matter what.

At the very least, that made him better than methamphetamines. Or heroin. Or any of the other things she either knew or suspected her mother had tried in her day. But even as she thought that, she could hear her sister's voice as if Fleurette was standing there beside her.

Are you really sure that "better than meth" is a decent recommendation?

Shut up, Fleurette, Julienne thought ferociously.

And then startled, there on the table, when the door to the room opened again. And Cristiano walked in.

His gaze met hers, and she hardly recognized what she saw there.

Beneath the glacial arrogance that was all Cristiano, there was something else. Something that made her hold her breath as he ventured near, nodding coldly at the doctor to continue.

Together they stared at the screen before them, and the unearthly picture that didn't seem to make sense—until it did.

Cristiano stood next to where she lay, and she stared up at him as his throat convulsed. Once, then again.

The doctor pointed out the baby's features, and Julienne looked from the screen to Cristiano's stricken expression. And at the hand that flexed slightly at his side. Then, following an urge that came straight from the swell of emotion in her heart that made it beat too hard and too loud, she dared to reach over and slide her hand into his.

She made a great show of looking at the screen, not at him while she did it.

Cristiano stiffened. Julienne expected him to shake her hand off.

But then, a breath later, his hand wrapped around hers. And held her fast.

That evening, Julienne dressed for dinner the way she always did. She smoothed her way into another stretchy dress, this one with a longer skirt that brushed the floor as she moved. It made her feel prettier somehow. Especially since the baby had been particularly active all day, kicking and punching like he had a score to settle.

"Or," she murmured, rubbing her belly as she walked out of her room and into the atrium, "like a little baby boy whose papa saw his face at last."

She could hardly put into words how that made her feel. It hadn't mattered to her that Cristiano had walked out with the doctor, and had not returned. Or it hadn't mattered *much*. Not when she could still feel the sensation of his hand on hers. The way he clenched so tight, and kept holding on to her even after they finished with the picture part of the examination.

Her fingers flexed of their own accord. And she could still feel the heat of his grip. The strength.

It was a beautiful spring evening and against her will, Julienne took a deep, almost happy sort of breath. She loved this villa more every day, though she tried so hard not to let it charm her. The graceful colonnade that formed the border of the atrium, wound with flowering vines. The atrium itself, a beautiful central garden that made every room in the house feel a part of the wild, surrounded by so much Tuscan beauty on both sides. She made her way down the path that cut from the guest suite to the formal part of the villa, with its many reception rooms. The stones beneath her feet were still warm from the day. The trees that stretched above her head provided a canopy of shade and birdsong. The small pond had a little fountain on one end, so the sound of water spilling and falling filled the whole of the villa like a happy song.

She couldn't help but smile as she made it to the dining room. But to her surprise, the table was not set. The housekeeper stood there instead, and nodded diffidently when she entered.

"Mr. Cassara requests the pleasure of your company on the west terrace," the housekeeper said.

Julienne wanted to argue. She wanted to demand that Cristiano come to her, and that they continue this tradition that she'd put into place when he'd left her here. Because maybe she wanted to play at being the lady of the manor—the lady of *this* manor, anyway.

His lady, something in her whispered.

She made herself smile at the waiting housekeeper, which was better than crying at her own foolishness. "We wouldn't want to keep Mr. Cassara waiting."

And she followed the housekeeper around to the west side of the villa, through one pretty, airy salon after the next. Eventually they walked out onto a stone terrace surrounded by wrought iron, also festooned with flowers and greenery. The terrace sat up above a slope of vineyard that rolled down into the valley below. It was not quite dark, and the light was magical, making the red rooftops of the villa's outbuildings and guest cottages gleam, while the marching pairs of cypress trees along the estate's winding lanes seemed to head straight for the setting sun.

She told herself the light was the reason Cristiano looked the way he did then, standing at the rail with all that soft gold licking over his strong, gloriously perfect body.

The body she knew better now, having refreshed her recollection of him last night.

And it amazed her that she could still blush after the things they'd done, but she did. Hard and hot. She hoped he would mistake it for another trick of the light.

He turned at her approach. And though his face was cast in shadow, then, she could still feel the impact of his intense gaze.

And everything felt fraught, suddenly. As if that intensity that emanated from him was part of the silky Tuscan golden light between them. And it was all around her, too, pressing in tight. Until she wasn't sure which one of them might burst.

She didn't know what to do. And the baby was kicking, her face was aflame and she could *feel* the way he looked at her, all that hunger and hope. Not that she imagined he'd admit that last part. She flexed her hand again, then she walked to him because she couldn't think of a single other thing to do.

And her heart stuttered as she drew close, because he reached out his hand and took hers.

Of his own volition this time.

And then, stunning her, he pulled her close.

"I thought we would eat here," Cristiano said, sounding formal and stuffy and delicious. And the way he gazed down at her, she was not entirely certain what sort of meal he meant. "To take advantage of the view."

Her head was tipped back so she could look him full in the face, though she had no memory of doing that of her own volition. "I like the view," she said softly.

His gaze dropped to her mouth, and she felt everything inside her shudder to life. Then bloom, in a riot of sensation and need.

But he did not kiss her.

"Thank you," Cristiano said instead, his voice like gravel. "I cannot describe to you what it was like to see the baby." That look in his gaze, as stricken as it had been earlier, sharpened. "My son."

And Julienne could blame her hormones all she liked, because it hardly mattered when the end result was the same. Her eyes welled up, then spilled over.

"Our baby," she whispered. "Our son."

And for a moment, there was nothing but the deep red and thick gold of the setting sun, his hands on hers, and the new life they'd made between them as they stood, not quite kissing.

Finally, she thought, a dangerous hope careening around inside of her.

Because she'd imagined this moment, but she'd never thought it would happen. Never.

And as if he knew they were discussing him, the baby kicked. Hard.

Julienne took Cristiano's hands in hers, then slid them down onto her belly. She pressed them in, smiling up at him as she waited. Then smiled even wider when the baby kicked.

"He's saying hello," she whispered. "To his father."

Cristiano jolted. Julienne could feel the electric charge go through him. And then his face changed. She saw a flash of wonder. His dark eyes lit up, and in that instant, he was…unguarded. Disarmed.

The baby kept kicking, and Cristiano's hands molded to her belly. She could feel all their heat and strength. She could feel the baby kicking. And she had the indescribable joy of watching a smile creep its way across Cristiano Cassara's austere face.

She could feel how wet her cheeks were, and it didn't occur to her to wipe them dry. Julienne could have stood where they were forever, and she wanted to—lost in this moment that felt as old as the hills and fields around them. A man and a woman and their coming child. She felt ancient. Connected to the earth, the seasons, every woman who'd come before her and all the women who would follow.

Julienne had understood that she'd gotten pregnant, of course. And she'd understood how. She had been overwhelmed by what that meant, for both of them. And apprehensive about his reaction.

But it was not until now, with only the soft, golden sunset in Tuscany as their witness, that she truly understood what it meant that she and Cristiano had *made a new life* together.

She felt her heart break open inside her chest, but it wasn't a heartbreak in the classic sense. It was more love, not less. It made more of her heart to go around, suddenly. All the shattered pieces fused back together, better than before.

More, not less.

"We did this," she whispered now. "You and me."

"This feels like a miracle, Julienne," he replied, his voice a mere thread of sound.

And then he broke her heart into pieces all over again, then stitched them back together in the same breath, as he sank down to his knees before her.

Julienne couldn't believe that any of this was happening. That she was here, with him, and that look on his face. That Cristiano was looking at her—or her belly, anyway—with so much tenderness. So much obvious, astonished delight. He spread his hands out to cover as much of her bump as he could, and then he leaned forward and placed a kiss there where his thumbs nearly met.

She couldn't stop crying, and she had never been quite so far from sad in all her life.

He looked up at her, this beautiful man, his eyes so bright they blocked out all that Tuscan gold. Like another miracle, right here on this terrace.

"We will marry," he said, a gruff command. "We must marry."

"I will marry you," she replied. "Of course, I'll marry you."

But it wasn't until she'd said it that she realized he hadn't exactly asked.

"He will be one of the good ones," Cristiano said fiercely. "I will see to it personally."

"He will be absolutely perfect," she agreed, because this was their son. And there were no curses, no poisoned blood. And the life inside her would turn into a boy who would never know the vile things others might predict about him. She would be his mother, and unlike her own, Julienne would make sure of it.

Cristiano stood then, this man she had loved for as long as she'd known him. First as a teenage girl with a crush, then as a hopeless employee he never once saw as a woman. And now, she knew all too well what it was like to have his mouth between her legs, his hands on her breasts, and best of all, the hardest part of him deep inside her, again and again.

And she loved him more.

Julienne wished that she could go back in time and tell that terrified sixteen-year-old how it would all turn out. That Cristiano would save her from the Boucher women's fate. That she would love him. That they would make a son together.

And then he would become her husband, and a father, and if there was a happier version of ever after, Julienne knew that neither she nor the teenage version of herself could possibly imagine it.

He led her over to the table she hadn't even seen, so lost was she in him. In this. He sat her down so she could look out at the vineyard, and the hills that rolled into forever, as the sun finally inched its way below the horizon.

This is everything you ever wanted, she kept telling herself, waiting for it to feel believable. Or real.

Beside her, Cristiano kept touching her belly, and even began speaking sternly to her bump, man to man.

She was so full to bursting, that it wasn't until later, when they'd eaten their dinner, and were sitting, enjoying the mild evening, that she realized one crucial thing was missing.

Cristiano had talked of parenting, and of marrying. He'd told her his plans of how it would be between them, and Julienne had agreed, but he had never once mentioned the most important thing of all.

Love.

CHAPTER TEN

"WE WILL MARRY at once," Cristiano announced the following morning, watching Julienne as she settled herself across from him, wearing nothing but the sheet they'd kicked off the bed early. His wife, he thought, with a stamp of possessive fire. The mother of the son he nearly hadn't gone to see—and had, in the end, because of that tenderness that only she brought out in him. It only made him more determined to move quickly now—before the realities of life as a Cassara set in, as he knew they would. They always did. And before that tender thing he could not put into words curdled and died like everything else he touched. "I will have a special license and priest here by nightfall."

"How romantic," she said dryly, and there was a flicker of something he couldn't say he liked in her toffee-colored eyes.

He studied her a moment, telling himself he was imagining things. This was the woman who had cried, she was so happy. And then cried for entirely different reasons in his bed all night.

"These are practicalities, Julienne," he said, aware that there were landmines here, though he couldn't understand why. "The sooner they are dealt with, the less we need speak of them."

"And, naturally, our only purpose here is to be practical." She shifted the sheet she'd wrapped around her, hiking it higher over her breasts. Cristiano wondered if she knew how very much she looked like a Roman goddess, toga and all. "While also having sex."

"Is that a complaint?"

She was looking out at the scenery, the rolling hills and the thicket of rosebushes. "I wouldn't dream of lodging a complaint. Besides, you don't care for my methods. Too scandalous."

"I thought we were in agreement," he said, mildly enough.

She looked different this morning, though he couldn't have said why. It wasn't the sheet or the fact she was sitting here on his private terrace, though that was certainly new and different. She had her hair up again, but in haphazard sort of pile instead of the sleek chignon that he recalled from the office. Maybe that was it. Maybe she no longer bothered with sleekness, which made him wonder why any woman did. When the other side of it was this—all soft woman, rosy cheeks and clear toffee eyes.

"I said I would marry you, yes," she said, and he realized after a beat that she was mimicking his own excessively mild tone. Exactly. "But there's no rush, surely. The world will not be ending at nightfall."

"I see no reason to wait."

"I cannot marry without my sister present." She shook her head at him, but at least that meant she was looking at him instead of out into the distance. "And don't you have a grandmother? Right here in Tuscany?"

Cristiano did not frown. Because he ordered himself not to frown. "Technically. But my grandmother would have no interest in attending my wedding. I'm not sure she would bother to attend my funeral, and of the two, it would likely bring her far greater joy."

Julienne laughed, but when he didn't join in—and, in fact, only stared at her implacably—she sobered. "You can't be serious."

"I know you have decided she is a sympathetic figure, Julienne, but my grandmother is an unpleasant woman. She takes pride in it. When I was a child, I was convinced that every fairy tale involving a witch and the forest was about her."

Julienne's gaze cooled, and too late, he remembered what she'd told him about the way the women in her family had been treated in France. And the way she had already come to his grandmother's defense. "You will forgive me, but can you really trust any stories you heard about her? Your grandfather was hardly an objective source."

Cristiano felt he should have received commendations for remaining calm in the face of such provocation. Medals, at the very least. But none appeared forthcoming, so he pinched his nose and wished for strength. "You are basing this on the letters you read, is that it?"

"The letters, yes, and the long-term marital affair that was celebrated in each and every one of those letters." Julienne's brows rose. "As the person you decided should marry you *tonight*, you should perhaps take note. I don't like cheaters or liars. And if my husband treated me the way your grandfather treated your grandmother, I would not waft off into the nearest forest and make myself into a fairy tale. I would burn him down."

He felt his gaze narrow. "Noted. But has it occurred to you that my grandfather was not the villain of this tale?"

"I understand why you want to believe that." Her throat worked, but it took her a moment to speak. "Then again, this is how men tell stories about women they can't control, isn't it? Whores. Witches."

"Wives?" he supplied, sardonically. Then regretted it when she turned that dark glare on him. He sighed. "Life is not black-and-white, especially when it comes to marriages. People are not all one thing or another."

"But in the case of your grandparents, one of them carried on an affair that went on for decades. The other lives by herself in a cottage, cut off from the world. One was considered a great man and celebrated internationally when he died. The other is loathed even by her own grandson." She shrugged. "It feels black-and-white, doesn't it?"

Cristiano studied the flush on her cheeks, realizing belatedly that it was temper. "Do you have grandparents too?" he asked. "Is that what this is about? Or is this something more prosaic than a sudden, deep concern for a woman you've never met...like second thoughts about a wedding, for example?"

Not that he would entertain her second thoughts.

"They say my grandmother died of shame," Julienne said, with a certain starkness that tore at him. "Not long after I was born. My grandfather had died when my mother was still young, which everyone agreed was a great blessing. Because he never had to know what became of her."

"And what of your father? Your father's family?"

"The man I think was my father also died, but no one is quite certain where he came from. Or if he left any family behind him. I've heard theories that his accent was Parisian by way of Marseille. But then again, some argued that he was very clearly not French at all. Who can say? All I know is, he overdosed when I was twelve, and I have never known how to feel about it, because I hardly knew him."

"I know my grandmother very little," Cristiano said, because every story she told him about her past was worse than the one before. And wasn't that the point of this? They would make something new. They would make it all better. "But it is enough."

"Is she a heroin addict?" Julienne asked, dryly. "I had heard many parts of the Cassara family legend, but not that."

Cristiano wanted to snap back at her, the way he would at an underling, but she no longer worked for him. Failing that, he wanted to get his hands on her and use the language they were both far more fluent in.

"I do not understand this intriguing take on a woman you've never met," he said, fighting to keep his voice calm. And not sure that he succeeded when her eyes flashed. "Surely you can allow for the possibility that I might be the expert on her motivations here? Since of the two of us, I'm the only one who knows her."

"Maybe your grandmother loved your grandfather to a distraction," Julienne said softly, and her pretty face was unreadable. "So much so that it drove her crazy when he met someone else. Have you ever stopped to think about that?"

"There will be a special license and a priest here by nightfall," Cristiano told her evenly. "Unless you have some further objection? Preferably not one that is based on your imaginary version of my grandmother?"

And when Julienne looked away, she did not look back for a very long time.

"I cannot marry without my sister here," she said again. "I won't."

"Then, *cara*, I would suggest you stop arguing about my grandparents' marriage and get her on a plane," Cristiano said silkily. "Because the wedding will happen. Tonight."

Fleurette arrived that evening, grumpier than usual, but with the same giant chip on her tattooed shoulder.

Julienne was so glad to see her, it hurt.

"You know you don't actually have to marry him, right?" Fleurette asked as she sat in Julienne's bedchamber in the guest suite with her, watching balefully as Julienne smoothed out the bodice of the dress that had appeared on her bed, as if by magic.

Not magic, she knew. Cristiano.

Cristiano, who could go to the trouble to pick out a beautiful dress for her to wear to what would no doubt be a beautiful wedding, but couldn't love her. Didn't love her.

Does he love anything? the voice inside her asked, sounding entirely too much like her sister. *Can he?*

"Why wouldn't I marry him?" Julienne asked, catching Fleurette's gaze in the mirror's reflection. And choosing to keep her thoughts on love to herself. "He's the father of my child. And as you've pointed out to me repeatedly over the past ten years, I have been hopeless about him from the start."

"I realize it gets confusing here in Europe," Fleurette said dryly. "But it is not necessary to marry a man simply because he got you pregnant. I know Italy *looks* medieval, but it's still the modern world here too, no matter the age of the buildings. No one cares anymore if a child is born out of wedlock."

"You don't care," Julienne corrected her quietly. "But that is not to say that others share your views."

Fleurette rolled her eyes. "Do I need to remind you that neither one of us was born on the right side of the blanket? We don't even have the same father."

"You don't know that. It's as likely that we have the same father as that we don't."

"This is the difference between us, Julienne," Fleurette said softly. Sadly. "You want so badly to believe there might be goodness in the world that you'll sacrifice yourself on the off chance you might find it. I know better. A sacrifice is a sacrifice. All it means is that you lose something."

And if Julienne could have, she would have bundled up her sister in cotton wool and made the world so good she would have no choice but to accept it—but that didn't work. She'd tried. And yes, it had worked out much better than planned, but Fleurette never forgot what could have happened that night in Monte Carlo. What would have happened if Julienne had approached a different man.

Sometimes Julienne thought it haunted her sister more than it haunted her.

"I want better for my son," Julienne said now. "I want to give him absolutely everything, and I don't need you to try to make me feel badly about that."

"I'm not trying to make you feel badly," Fleurette said, her voice tight. "I came, didn't I? I'm wearing a pastel dress that makes me feel dead inside. I'm perfectly appropriate and ready to applaud. But I'm also your sister."

"Fleurette. Please."

"And you once sacrificed yourself *for me*, so I think you can do me the courtesy of listening to me. I'm not asking you to hide in an alley and save yourself."

Julienne met her sister's gaze in the mirror. And it was there between them, the way it always was. That same dark night. What she'd been prepared to do. What Fleurette would have had to live with. The ghost of what could have been.

She found she couldn't speak, so she nodded. Jerkily.

"I don't think you're doing any of this for the right reasons," Fleurette said. Julienne said nothing, but rubbed her belly ostentatiously. Her sister rolled her eyes. "Yes, I'm aware that you're pregnant. But I think you want to wrap all of this up in a pretty little bow. You saved yourself for this man. You ranted on and on about bookends, and then you went out of your way to make it happen. I don't want to speculate how you ended up pregnant."

"The usual way, I assure you."

Another eye roll. "My point is, we got a raw deal. We never had a chance. If you'd walked up to any other man in that bar, neither one of us would be standing here right now. We both know where we'd be, if not the precise street address."

"Do you think I don't think about that every day?"

"I know you do." Fleurette's voice and gaze were intense. "And I understand why you want this to be neat. Tidy. If you marry the man who saved us all those years ago, does it wipe the slate clean? If you have his baby, and live with him, do you wash all the sin away?"

"Because it can't possibly be true that I love him."

But Julienne's voice sounded tinny and hollow, and there was a great weight deep in her belly that felt too much like a stone.

"Maybe you love him and maybe you don't," Fleurette said, her undertone something like urgent. "Maybe you've confused love with a sense of obligation. But none of that matters."

"It matters to me quite a lot, actually."

"Julienne, you deserve someone who loves *you*," Fleurette said, scowling at her. "You deserve to be loved, full stop. You deserve someone who loves every single thing about you, always. Someone who does not require acts of sacrifice in return for simply not being disgusting in a bar ten years ago. You've spent a life surviving and sacrificing—for me, for us, for your baby. But what about you? What would happen if you lived *for you* instead?"

"I've never felt more alive in my life," Julienne threw at her. "Ever."

And she expected her sister to fight back, but she didn't. She only held Julienne's gaze for a long, long time, then nodded.

"Then I'm thrilled to be here to celebrate you," she said quietly.

But Julienne couldn't get those words out of her head. *What about you?*

Fleurette did not disrupt the wedding, as promised. And Julienne couldn't have said why there was a part of her that found that disappointing. Did she want the excuse?

You want an enemy, came that voice inside, again sounding too much like the too-wise Fleurette. *You want to fight your way into this marriage, and better still, have something to fight against.*

And she found her hands were damp as she walked along the colonnade, and out to meet her fate. Her husband. With no enemies and no fights.

It was a quiet, simple affair, out on the terrace where Cristiano had gone down to his knees and kissed her baby. His baby.

Our baby, she thought fiercely.

It was quiet, simple, and fast. The priest intoned their vows, they both responded appropriately, and then Julienne watched as if from a great distance as Cristiano slid a pair of rings onto her hand. He provided her with one to put on his hand in return.

And then it was done.

She was married to Cristiano Cassara. Just as she'd always dreamed.

There was a small, pleasant dinner. Then Fleurette took her leave, and the sisters stared at each other. Neither one mentioning how strange it was that Fleurette had flown across the planet to witness a decidedly unromantic wedding ceremony and wasn't even staying the night.

"I love you," Fleurette said fiercely, and hugged her, hard. "Always."

"I love you too," Julienne replied.

She waited until she heard the helicopter blades begin to whir. She watched it rise into the air to whisk Fleurette back to an airfield outside of Florence, where one of the Cassara jets waited for her.

Then she went back into the villa, a married woman, to find her husband waiting for her.

She should have been dancing for joy. Or at least simmering with it, somewhere inside. She wore a lovely white dress. She had his rings on her finger. And when she came into the salon where he waited, staring down at one of those tumblers of whiskey he never drank, he gazed at her with a look on his face that she could only describe as possessive.

This was what she'd wanted.

Wasn't it?

"I've taken the liberty of moving your things into the master bedroom," he told her in his calm, certain way. "And now, wife, I think it is time we consummate this marriage. Unless you would like to take this opportunity to further debate my grandparents' marriage."

She wanted to smile, but her mouth felt funny. "I would not."

Cristiano's smile was not funny at all. It was savage. Erotic.

He swept her into his arms, lifting her as if she weighed nothing at all though she was seven months pregnant. He carried her through the villa, then bore her into the master bedroom, where he lay her down on the bed as if she was fragile.

And wasn't that a funny thing, because she certainly felt fragile.

His mouth was demanding on hers, and it didn't matter what oddities she felt in her heart tonight, because her body was his.

Always, only, and ever his.

His hands moved over her, as if he was learning her anew. As if the fact she was now *his wife* made her a stranger he needed to reacquaint himself with. Inch by inch.

She wanted to burst into tears, or let out a terrible sob she wasn't sure would ever end. Instead, she poured it into her own kisses. She took it out on his body, peeling off the gorgeously tailored suit he wore to find the glory of his flesh beneath.

And this time, he lifted her to straddle him and then watched her as she rode them both toward that bliss, his eyes a fierce claiming all their own.

She sobbed all right, passion and that odd stone inside her together making her too raw to do anything but let it out. Again and again and again.

And she loved him. And she was married to him now. And somehow, she had to come to terms with what all of that meant.

Because it wasn't what she thought it would mean, back when she'd fantasized about things like this. About him.

He poured himself into her, and then they lay there together. They both fought to catch their breath as the breeze came in through the windows smelling of jasmine, the deep green of growing things and the dark brown earth, and the faintest touch of rosemary.

She thought about bookends. She thought about that dark, grim life she and Fleurette had escaped in the hills of France. She thought about that awful bus ride down into Monte Carlo with the last of their euros, the stolen dress and the longest walk of her life into that hotel bar.

"You deserve to be loved," Fleurette had said.

And maybe, just maybe, Julienne also deserved to ask for more. Instead of simply accepting what came her way and thinking that was the height of what life had to offer. She understood his grandmother, that was the thing. She understood the decision to live as she liked, to be *alive*, even if it meant living all alone in exile and scaring children while she did it. Just because most women didn't make that choice didn't mean she couldn't feel the temptation of it, like another bit of jasmine in the air, blooming just for her.

"Cristiano," she said, as much to the dark ceiling above her as to the man who lay beside her. The man who had married her in haste, despite the fact everyone knew how that went, traditionally. But would he be the one doing the repenting? Or would she? "Husband."

"Wife," he said, as if in agreement.

She shifted to look at him, propping herself up on her elbow and wishing her belly didn't make her feel quite so ungainly.

"Why do you look so serious?" he asked. "Everything is settled now. You and me. Our son. If you truly wish it, I will introduce you to my grandmother, though I will have to insist you maintain a reasonable distance. You never know if she'll throw things."

"I love you," she said, and she could hear the foreboding in her own voice. The worry. But she said it, and that startled, thunderstruck look on his face didn't make her take it back. "I love you, Cristiano. I always have. I loved you when I was a teenager you happened to save, and I loved you as a businesswoman who sought your good opinion in the office. I loved you when I came to you in that hotel six months ago, and I loved you even before you recognized our son. I have loved you a thousand ways already, and I imagine I will love you in a thousand more before we're done."

And she wasn't surprised when all he did was stare at her, his expression arrested. Frozen, almost.

Hurt, yes. But not surprised.

"You deserve someone who loves you," Fleurette had said so fiercely.

"There's no need to talk of love," he said, sounding as if he was being strangled.

"Of course there's a need," she said, and it was hard to keep her voice soft. To keep her gaze on his, when he looked very nearly horrified and her heart ached the way it did. "Love is the entire point, Cristiano."

"No," Cristiano said in a low voice. And this time, when he broke her heart, it was a devastation. "*Cara.* Julienne. Don't do this. Surely you, of all people, must know that love is a lie."

CHAPTER ELEVEN

FINALLY EVERYTHING WAS going according to plan.

Cristiano might not have originally planned to marry and have children, but now that one was done and the other imminent, he found he rather liked the surprising peace of domesticity. It was far better than being haunted. And the new plan made sense.

He gave up his sleek, modern penthouse and moved back into the house he'd once given to Julienne and her sister. It was a home, not a bachelor's residence, and he liked the idea of his son playing in the garden, or tearing up and down the stairs. Especially once he bought the attached house next door and began making plans to create one, far better home for his family.

His family.

He liked that word, even if he only admitted that to himself privately.

But then, he liked having Julienne there, in his house. With him. He particularly liked her in his bed.

Even if she did have a terrible habit of speaking about love. Of all things.

He could not have picked words to describe the things he felt and if he did, he would have chosen other ones. That terrible, wrecking tenderness that swamped him when he touched her, or when he thought of the baby she carried. The weakness he felt in him at the sight of her.

"Of course your father loves you," his mother had told him when he was still small, but old enough to know better. *"He loves both of us. He struggles to show it, that's all."*

What was *love* but a tiny word that served as a gateway to despair?

Their wedding night, she'd stared at him with those eyes of hers he liked to think of as the precise shade of Cassara's finest toffee. Though that night, there had been a shine to them that had trickled into his gut, kicked around in there and made him…edgy.

"Imagine if your father had loved your mother," she'd said. "And if your grandfather had loved your grandmother. Who would you be now, do you think?"

"I respect you," he had growled in return, shifting closer to her so he could put his hands on her body. And once again, speak to her in terms they both understood completely. "I want you. I will raise our son the way my grandfather raised me."

"To be happy?" she had asked in her quiet way. "No matter who it hurts?"

"To be good," he had retorted, feeling unaccountably challenged.

But he had handled it the way he dealt with all things involving Julienne.

With his mouth, his hands. With the near inexpressible pleasure of burying himself deep inside of her.

And as far as he was concerned, the conversation was over.

He moved them back to Milan, installing her in his house. His bed. Right where he wanted her—with the added bonus of it being *her*. Julienne Boucher, the most formidable of all his vice presidents. Cristiano rather liked that he could come home from work and actually discuss it with her, because her opinion was always learned, careful and most of the time, right.

The research that Massimo had provided him, on pregnancy, parenthood and everything else he knew he would have to contend with, and soon, suggested that a woman's preferences might change once she became a mother. Then again, they might not. He was happy enough to let Julienne do as she pleased, but he couldn't help hoping that what would please her most would be—after an appropriate amount of leave—to join him at the Cassara Corporation again.

"Because it is not nepotism if we're already married?" she asked one night, as she sat in the bedroom that was now theirs. She was rubbing lotion into her enormous belly in an attempt to control her stretch marks, a job that Cristiano sometimes took upon himself, because there was no part of her he didn't find beautiful. Marks and all.

Tonight, he only watched. His wife and the son he would meet soon enough. Sometimes the sight of her so close to giving birth made his heart careen about dangerously in his chest.

Appropriate anxiety, he assured himself. It was what anyone would feel.

"Nothing inappropriate happened between us while you were my subordinate," he said, with a shrug. "And I would be a fool indeed not to take advantage of the fact that one of the greatest minds that has ever worked for the company has returned to me."

"To you, Cristiano," she said, in that mild way she always used these days. That cool, calm voice while something too dark for comfort gleamed in her gaze. "I came back to Italy to tell you that you are to be a father. Not to concern myself with bolstering your corporate profile."

He didn't like her tone. But he only gazed back at her. "I fail to see why it cannot be both."

She stopped rubbing the lotion into her skin, and put the top back on the jar of the thick salve she was using. He couldn't help but think that her movements were jerky.

"Surely the benefits of marrying a man of your wealth and consequence is that I need not concern myself with work." And though there was no hint of temper on her face, he felt it in the air between them, anyway. "If I, for example, wish to do nothing at all but welcome our son into the world by loving him fiercely, wholeheartedly and with singular focus, that should be fine, shouldn't it?"

"I wasn't aware that you had to choose between the two," he replied. "That is the true benefit of marrying me. You don't have to choose a thing. You can have it all, whatever you like."

"Not quite *whatever* I like." And her eyes were on him in a way that made him…distinctly uncomfortable. "You don't believe in love. Why pretend you can offer me things you can't, Cristiano?"

She launched herself from the bed, one hand going to support the small of her back as she moved, and then she swept out of the bedroom. Leaving him there.

To think about her obsession with *love*.

And that was not the first inkling he'd had that

all was not quite as rosy for his new wife as he'd imagined. But it was most direct.

Julienne never denied him. At night, their passion only seemed to grow, wilder and hotter, even as they moved into her final stage of pregnancy. And she always cried out his name in that same perfect song.

She indulged him when he wanted to get his hands on her bump, or put his mouth there so he could speak to his son.

But they were not far off from her due date when he realized that it wasn't that there was a different light in her eyes when she looked at him these days. It was that there was an absence of light.

He didn't know how he could have missed it.

And what made it worse was that he didn't figure out what it was that was getting so deeply beneath his skin until Fleurette appeared, in her usual defiant state, a few days before Julienne was due.

"I can't miss the birth of my nephew," Fleurette announced when she saw him, and *her* gaze, Cristiano could not help but notice, was bright and hot and not particularly friendly. "I won't."

"Of course not," he murmured.

And then he'd been called upon to handle a near disaster at one of their processing facilities. He'd spent all day handling the various politics between his plant manager and the local government in that country, and a full contingent of his attorneys.

When he arrived home, it was late. He was surprised to find lights still on, when Julienne had taken to a far earlier bedtime these days.

He nodded at his housekeeper as he entered, accepting the mail and messages she'd prepared for him.

And then he drifted further into the house, following a sound he'd very rarely heard here.

Had never heard here, or any place he'd ever lived in Milan, if he was honest.

Laughter.

He loosened his tie as he followed the surprising burst of it, past the study and the rooms he normally used to the small salon Julienne had claimed as her own in the back of the house. In the month that she had lived with him here, she had slowly substituted some of the furnishings, making it less a random collection of items a designer had chosen, and more hers.

Tonight, as he stood at the threshold, out in the dark hall beyond, the first thing he noticed was the light.

Endless, glorious light, and not only from the lamps she'd lit.

It was all over her face. Julienne sat in a comfortable armchair that she'd told him would be perfect for nursing his son. Before her, Fleurette was telling a story, sitting cross-legged on the floor gesticulating widely while also doing something with Julienne's feet.

Painting her nails, he realized in the next moment. Or supposedly painting them, when she wasn't waving her arms about.

And Julienne looked…*alive*.

Her eyes shone, sweet and bright, all toffee and no darkness. Her face was filled with laughter, and hope and that astonishing quicksilver song he only heard when he was deep inside her and she was calling out his name.

Cristiano felt his heart flip in his chest, as if heralding a cardiac event.

He felt frozen where he stood, staring at this woman. His wife. As if he'd never seen her before.

Perhaps you haven't, a dark voice inside him suggested. *Why would you deserve her?*

He didn't think he made a sound, so caught was he in all her brightness. The glorious shine of it.

Cristiano could have stared at her forever. He felt thirsty. Ravenous. And only that light and joy she generated could make it better. Could make *him* better.

But that was when she turned, saw him standing there and blinked.

"Cristiano," she said, her voice changing. And her face changing with it. "I didn't hear you come in."

And he watched, feeling as if there was a

hatchet buried deep in his chest, as all that light dimmed.

As if looking at him switched it off, that quickly.

Something in him thudded then, unpleasantly.

"I only just arrived," he heard himself say.

He glanced at her sister, but Fleurette's face was studiously blank. A condemnation in itself.

Cristiano felt his pulse kick in when he looked back at Julienne, because she was looking at him the exact same way she had since the night of their wedding. Calmly, yes. Coolly, even.

But with no trace whatsoever of all that glorious light.

"I will not disturb you," he said shortly, and left them there.

He went to his office in the house, but he couldn't focus on the work he needed to do, no matter how long he sat at his desk. And when he stopped pretending to work and stared at a shot of whiskey instead, daring himself to truly become his father once and for all, there was something in him that longed for the oblivion.

More than usual.

It would be so much easier *not* to feel anything. He could imagine it so clearly.

But he didn't take the drink. He didn't take the easy way out.

And when he climbed the stairs to the master bedroom and found Julienne there, he felt his heart stutter inside him when she looked at him in that same mild, empty way.

"Your sister being here makes you very happy," he said, studying Julienne's face for signs of… something. Something to stave off this panicked thing inside him.

"She's not really my sister. Or not only my sister. She's also my best friend." Her gaze rested on him. "And she loves me with every last cell in her body."

"Because you rescued her," Cristiano said.

And he saw a flash of *something* across her face then, but it wasn't that same light he'd seen earlier. It was temper.

But it was better than nothing.

And even as he thought that, it occurred to him that he felt most connected to Julienne—the person, if he was honest, he felt most connected to on the planet—through passion. Whether that passion was based in anger or desire, it was the only language he knew.

It was the only vocabulary he possessed.

And so perhaps it was not surprising that he felt something far too close to bereft as he watched her fight it back.

"You don't love someone because they do things for you," Julienne said, and though her gaze was hard on his, her voice was resolute. "You love them. That's all. And if a situation arises where you can do something for them, then you do it. But it's not a transaction."

And Cristiano understood, in a sickening flash, that transactions were all he knew.

That the people who had raised him had taught him passion, and he had equated it with their brand of drama. Theatrics. Operatic displays, cruelty and fiery conclusions.

He stared at this woman, ripe and round with his child, and for the first time in his life, Cristiano didn't have the slightest idea what to do. How to reach her, or find a way back to that beautiful light of hers that he was very much afraid he had already extinguished.

And this time he didn't think he could ignore the uncertainty and make it go away.

"I see how you're looking at me," Julienne said, and didn't quite roll her eyes. Because she was not her sister. Not yet. "Don't worry. I'm not going to ask anything of you that you can't give, Cristiano. I married you knowing exactly who you are."

And a week ago, a month ago, he might have accepted that. He might have nodded, thought that sounded like a perfectly reasonable bargain and carried on.

Tonight, those words sounded like an indictment.

But everything was different now.

Because *she* was different, and he had made her that way, and he wasn't sure that he could stand it.

He moved toward her, getting his hands on her body. Filling his fingers with the thick fall of her pretty hair, and then taking her mouth with his.

Because these were the only words he knew. This was the only passion that made sense to him.

This was the only way that he could make her sing with joy, for him.

And he proved it, to himself and to her, over and over again that night.

But in the morning, he left her with her sister, entirely too aware of the way she only seemed to relax once Fleurette was near. And he knew that as soon as the door closed behind him, she would once again light up the way she hadn't for him— not since their wedding.

And it was with a sense of fatalism, or possibly surrender—not that he'd ever had such a sensation before—that instead of going into his office, he went to Tuscany.

When the helicopter delivered him to his usual spot near the villa, he did not go inside. He took one of the property's hardy SUVs instead, and drove out into the hills.

An hour or so later, he wound around on a bumpy dirt lane, having left the cultivated part of the Cassara fields behind some time ago. And there the cottage sat, right where he remembered it, solid and defiant in the middle of nowhere.

Summer was coming, and the clearing where the cottage stood was carpeted with wildflowers. He walked toward the front of the small home, lecturing himself on the strange prickling he felt all over his body. It was not a wicked enchantment. She was not a witch.

Those had been the fancies of the boy he'd been, who'd been taught to hate her.

And it was only when he drew close that he realized that she was there. Right there. Folded into a chair on the front porch, watching his approach.

She looked wrinkled and wise, but her dark eyes still burned. She was dressed all in black, though he doubted very much that was any kind of nod to her widowhood. Her hands were like claws, her knuckles large as they clutched the head of her cane.

"You have the look of a salesman about you," she said, and her voice was precisely as he recalled it. More robust than a woman should sound on the cusp of ninety, to his way of thinking, and threaded through with a deep and abiding dislike. "A Cassara salesman, no less. The very worst kind."

"Hello, Grandmother," he replied.

The old woman sniffed. "Whatever it is you've come to say, I'm not interested. I do not require assistance. I do not wish to be placed in a home with other old people. I will die as I have lived here, happily alone and usually left to my own devices—as God intended."

"I didn't come here to put you in a home. Or argue with you, for that matter."

But it seemed she was making a list. "My health is none of your business, but it is excellent, since you've come looking. If you wish to develop this land, you will have to do so over my dead body. But never fear. I may be thriving at the moment but an old woman can only live so long. You may have to learn to wait for what you want—a trait no man in your family has ever possessed."

"I don't need your land. For God's sake."

"The last time you were here, boy, I thought I might make you cry. Is that why you returned? To test yourself against childhood nightmares? I'm delighted to try again."

She laughed and that part he remembered too well. Because it wasn't the demure, carefully cultivated laughter of the women he'd always known. He'd considered it unhinged when he'd been younger. But now, he understood.

It was joy. Pure joy, the kind Julienne shared with her sister and never him. It was uncontrolled. Untamed.

This is how men tell stories about women they can't control, Julienne had told him. *Whores. Witches.*

His grandfather had made his wife into a witch. How had Cristiano never seen that? And Piero was the one who had been heralded as a hero upon his death. When what he'd been was a selfish man who did as he liked. Who selected the people he would care for—Sofia Tomasi, Cristiano—and discarded those he disdained, like the woman he'd married and his only remaining son.

Nor had he ever seemed unduly concerned about the consequences.

It was like a mountain crumbling on top of him, sucking him under and crushing him there.

And Cristiano understood, with a pang of a deep, harsh grief, that this take on his beloved grandfather was not something he could unknow. It was not something he could pretend he hadn't seen.

"I do not think I will cry," he said to the grandmother he should have known all these years, his voice low. "If I am honest, I would sooner dig out my eyes and feed them to the crows."

She hooted derisively. "What do crows want with a rich man's eyes?"

He should not have been here, no matter what revelations might have come to him overnight. Making this her problem was proving that he was like all the rest of his family. That he was just like them, selfish to the core.

Cristiano had no idea what he hoped to gain.

But he stayed where he was, there on the porch of this cottage he'd avoided for most of his life.

"Grandmother," he said, with a stiff formality that in no way matched the moment but he thought she deserved nonetheless. "I've come to talk to you about love."

"Love?" The old woman cackled. "Your father was a drunk and his father a liar. They raised you in their spitting image. Too rich, too pampered and cruel with it. What can you possibly know of love?"

He didn't flinch away from the glare she settled on him.

"Nothing at all," he said quietly.

His grandmother studied him for what felt to Cristiano like a very long time. A lifetime, perhaps. The lifetime he might have known this woman, if things had been different. If his grandfather had been the hero Cristiano had always seen in him, instead of the man he was.

"If there is no love, there is no life," she said at last, and again he had the sense of some enchantment after all. Some spell she was casting as she spoke, and not because she was a witch. But because she might well be magic. "You can live on, mind. But it's nothing but going through the motions. I would not have imagined a Cassara would care about this distinction. You don't have to be fully alive to count all the money, after all."

"I have a wife," Cristiano heard himself say, as if the words were torn from somewhere deep inside him. Torn from the mouth of a version of himself he had never been—a version of himself who did things like ask for advice. "She says she loves me."

This old woman looked at him with canny, clever eyes, as if she'd known him all his life. And knew him better than he knew himself.

"But you, naturally, cannot be asked to concern yourself with the petty concerns of the heart. Not when you have sweet things to shove down throats. Sugar in place of character will never end well, boy. What do you want me to do? Build your poor wife a cottage next door? Or direct her to a coffin like your mother's?" And there wasn't the faintest trace of age in the look she leveled on him, then. "Those are the only two options for Cassara wives, as I understand it."

Cristiano did not argue, though he wanted to. Desperately.

"There has to be a third option," he said, his voice gruff. "There has to be."

"There is." His grandmother lifted her cane and pointed it at him. "You. Change yourself, boy. Not her. She's changed enough already if she's with you."

CHAPTER TWELVE

WHEN THE DOOR to her bedroom swung open, Julienne told herself that she was prepared.

Because what had this last month or so since their wedding been if not an exercise in preparation?

She arranged her face in a polite smile. She'd become good at it, she thought. She would remain calm and cool no matter what. She would not give up, the way his grandmother had, no matter the provocation. She was not sacrificing herself, no matter what Fleurette thought, she was *choosing*—

But the usual litany she chanted at herself blew away like smoke.

Because the man who came to the door was not her husband.

It was Cristiano, but a version of him she had not seen in a long time.

Not since that night in Monte Carlo, in fact. The second time around, when he had proven to her that, in truth, she hardly knew him at all.

He'd proven it again and again, deliciously.

And that's the reason you're in this state now, she reminded herself tartly. *About to have a baby in a marriage that feels like you're choking and drowning, daily.*

She might have resolved to live with it. But the man who slammed the bedroom door behind him made her jump a bit, there in their bed where she was propped up against the pillows, supposedly reading a book on breastfeeding.

"What has happened?" she asked, staring at him.

And Julienne was unable, in the face of all the ferocity she saw in him, to keep her tone even at all. The way she'd been doing since their brusque wedding, because it was that or start screaming. And she was afraid that once she started screaming she wouldn't stop. She'd felt it claw in her, those screams she wouldn't let loose, when she'd told him she loved him and he'd told her love was a lie.

A lie.

And had very clearly meant it.

"I've been to Tuscany," Cristiano said, and his voice wasn't his. Not really. It was gruff, dark. But there was a different undercurrent. It was one she didn't know.

"Did something happen to the villa?"

"Villa Cassara has stood for hundreds of years.

It will stand forever. And in any case, I didn't go to the villa."

"Cristiano." She used the repressive tone she sometimes employed on her sister, and it had about the same effect. One of his arrogant brows rose, with no hint of repentance. "I can't tell if something is wrong or not. Is it?"

"Something is terribly wrong," he told her, dark and urgent. "You are wrong."

He might as well have hauled off and punched her in the belly. Julienne felt her jaw drop open, even as in the next moment she told herself that she *absolutely refused* to give him the satisfaction of seeing her react like that. Or at all.

"Perhaps you missed the news," she managed to say crisply. "I have married a Cassara. I think you know full well that's a fast track to wrongness." She inclined her head in a fair mockery of the aristocratic way he did it. "I will accept your condolences."

"You have changed, Julienne."

He moved closer to the bed, where she'd been agitatedly turning pages in her book but failing to read a single word. Because the office had called, looking for him, and that told her only that he was off doing something he didn't want anyone to know about.

Had it started already? Was he off looking for his own long-term mistress to install in the house and push her out? Or had he lost himself in the whiskey she'd seen he'd left out on his desk, in an imitation of the father he hated and feared becoming?

And what did it say about her that she wasn't entirely sure which route was worse?

Then his words penetrated and she frowned. "I don't think I've changed. Perhaps you have. Or, more likely, you're paying more attention than you did before because we're living in the same house."

"No," he replied sternly, in that tone she recalled from the office. The one that brooked absolutely no argument. "There's a sadness in your eyes all the time now. Do you think I don't see it?"

"I'm sure you're mistaken. And I'm equally sure that you don't really care. Because if you did, you might have mentioned your thoughts on love before getting married."

Julienne had not meant to say that.

She was horrified that she'd said that.

She flushed, and hated the fact that she was so big now that she couldn't simply leap to her feet and walk away from her own embarrassment. Not without a struggle. Instead, she had to stay where she was, anchored to the bed by her giant belly.

By the child she was bringing into this mess. Into the arms of a man who didn't believe in love. It was bad enough for her. What would it do to their son?

Then again, she already knew. Cristiano was a walking advertisement for exactly what would happen.

"It doesn't matter now," she said, nervously, because she couldn't read that intense expression on his face. He seemed even more austere than usual. Almost as if he was in pain. And she could not bear that. "We are married. Our son will be here soon enough. We can love him, instead."

Or I will, she promised the baby. *I will love you enough for both of us.*

"I went to see my grandmother," he said as he came to a stop at the foot of the bed.

And had he said that he had personally flown himself to the moon and back, Julienne could not possibly have been more surprised.

"Your grandmother?" She gaped at him. "The fairy-tale witch?"

"Her name is Paola DeMarco." His voice was gruff again, his face grim. "She does not use her married name, which will perhaps not surprise you."

"Why did you go to see her?" Julienne asked. The baby kicked, hard enough to make her wince. And she told herself that was why her heart began to pound. "Did she cast a spell on you after all?"

"Because you spoke to me of whores and witches." And that grimness on his face began to look…ravaged, instead. "You made me question who it was who told me that particular fairy tale, and why. And because you married me and began at once to fade. And I want you to understand this, if nothing else, Julienne. I have no intention of repeating any of this history."

"I told you I would burn it to the ground," Julienne told him fiercely, thinking of that cold, sick feeling in her belly when his office had called. And the gloating letters from his grandfather's mistress. "I meant it."

His gaze on hers was savage. And beautiful. "There is nothing to burn save the empty, hollow carcass of the man I was before I met you."

And there was no pretending, then, that her heart wasn't beating hard and mad for him.

For hope.

But she couldn't seem to make herself speak.

"I told myself all was well," Cristiano said in that same tone. "And I wanted to believe it. But all the while, you looked at me through a stranger's eyes. No light. No joy. And in all the time I have known you, Julienne, you have never looked at me like that."

"You don't have to do this," she managed to get out. "Really."

And there was a kind of panic in her then. She fought against it, trying to roll herself out of the nest she'd made of too many pillows, but then he was there.

Cristiano was at the side of the bed, and then he was sitting there beside her. And this time, he didn't put his hands on her belly, or address himself to her bump.

He took her hands. And he looked into her eyes.

"Last night I came upon you laughing with your sister," he said, and she'd never heard him sound like this. Gravel and ice, certainly, but something hot and alive beneath. "And I couldn't help but think to myself that I had extinguished all that light. All that joy. Because when you look at me now, there's nothing but heartbreak on your face. And *tesoro mio*, you must know that I cannot bear for you to be broken. *I cannot bear it.*"

Julienne wanted to reach out to him. She wanted to fix this, whatever it was. It was as if the ice in him had cracked at last, she realized. And what she was seeing was the man beneath it.

Uncontrolled. Untamed.

Real, a voice in her whispered.

Cristiano kept going, his hands on hers. "My whole life I have equated emotion with pain. Terror. Grief and loss. The deeper the emotion, the more passion in its display, and the worse it has always been. I have watched a man I respected act as if what he'd done to his wife was something she deserved. That she'd brought upon herself. He was *proud* of it."

He shook his head, a cynicism she'd never seen

before in his gaze, not when he spoke of his beloved grandfather. And Julienne didn't entirely understand how she could feel all that same cynicism when it came to Piero Cassara, but want to soothe it away from Cristiano. With her hands, her mouth, whatever worked.

But he was still speaking, intent and low. "And I watched another man I never respected abuse my mother, who, it must be said, put more energy into martyring herself to her marriage than she ever did into raising her own child. These were the emotions I knew growing up. This was the passion that marked the Cassara family. Of course I told you that love was a lie. Do you know the only person who ever used that word in my hearing?" His mouth, firm and hard, thinned into grimness again. "Sofia Tomasi, the housekeeper who welcomed my grandmother into the Villa when Paola was a shy eighteen-year-old bride. Sofia loved my father, or so she liked to tell me, and she showed that love by undermining my grandmother at every turn. Pretending to befriend her and then using her confidences against her."

He shook his head, but the gaze he kept trained on her was fierce. "Every example of love I have ever seen has been a lie, Julienne. Save yours."

And his hands were on hers, so she gripped him, hard. She didn't care about the wetness on her cheeks, not as long as she could keep looking at him. At his face, torn apart by something deep and strong. *Ravaged,* she thought again.

She would take from him in an instant if she could. If only she could.

"You have loved me unwaveringly," Cristiano said and there was a kind of wonder in his voice. "You loved me when I was a bitter, angry man who had just sent his own parents to their deaths."

She did her best not to shout, *That is not your fault.*

He shifted, his fingers laced with hers now. "That you are so fierce about that is only further testament to the kind of person you are. You loved me then, Julienne. You loved me when I threw you and your sister into this house, then threw money at you to assuage my guilt, and did absolutely nothing to help you make your way in the world."

"Aside from paying for it."

"Money does not keep anyone warm, try as they might," he growled.

And it was her turn to smile, through the tears that blurred her vision. "Cristiano. I do love you. I have always loved you. But please, take it from me, the money to pay a heating bill in a cold winter keeps anyone warm enough. Everything else is icing on the cake."

He reached over and traced that smile on her mouth with his fingers, as if it was a priceless work of art. As if she was.

"That smile."

And his voice was so intense, then, it nearly hurt to hear him. Nearly. Instead, she melted.

"I have missed that smile."

"Cristiano—"

"That you love me at all humbles me," he told her, as if he was making vows. And not with the briskness he'd displayed at their wedding. "You, who have been through so much. I thought that the purpose of my life was to distinguish myself from my father. I wanted so desperately to be nothing like him. But somehow, I never saw that I was as drunk on my own perceived virtue as he ever was on whiskey. Until you."

"None of this is necessary. Really."

"It is more than necessary." And his voice was like thunder, then. "It is past due. This whole time, I have thought that I could avoid saying these words that I barely know how to form if I expressed myself another way. I thought that while I heard that beautiful song of yours, so passionate and all mine, you would hear the truth in my heart as well."

Julienne found she was holding her breath.

"The things you make me feel terrify me," he said, and she understood that she was seeing the real Cristiano now. No ice. All flesh and man. And all hers. "They make me feel mortal, weak and wrong. And all my life, I have considered it my duty to exorcise anything I felt. Better to be like ice. Better by far to be half-dead—but you make me feel alive, Julienne. You forced me, against my will and inclination, to face up to the things I wanted so badly I'd locked them away inside myself. And then you systematically broke down each and every one of my compartments."

She didn't know if she should melt or apologize. But Cristiano took one of her hands and brought it to his chest. Then placed her palm over his heart. "I'm going to tell you a fairy tale."

"Does it involve witches?" she managed to ask, not sure if she was laughing or crying.

With his free hand, he reached over and wiped away the water beneath her eyes.

"Once upon a time there was a fool," he told her, his voice a low rumble that she could feel, now, as well as hear. "He was raised by an ogre and a troll. The ogre taught him airs and graces. The troll taught him pain. The fool knew no better, and imagined that one was a king and the other a jailer."

"This is already a very sad story."

Cristiano's dark eyes gleamed, but he kept on. "Time went on, and the fool allowed his king to color his world. He thought that made him a man. A hero, even. Until one day, at the end of a very low hour when he had indulged his innate selfishness and would soon learn that there would be consequences for his folly, he had the opportunity instead to play the hero he'd always imagined he was. For in walked a girl, and he saved her."

"Oh, okay," she said. "I like *this* story."

"But you see, like any fool, he thought saving her was enough. He turned his back on her, told himself it was a virtue and made a career out of turning himself to stone."

Beneath her hand, his heart beat, hard and strong. Beautiful. And inside her, she felt their son's feet poke at her, and if this wasn't love—physical and real and true—she was sure she didn't know the meaning of the word.

"And then one day, years later, the girl found him again," Cristiano said, still telling his story. Or maybe this was really their story. "She flattered him, flirted with him. For she had grown up to become a beautiful princess, and the fool thought—*of course*. He considered himself a hero, so why shouldn't he have a princess? So he kissed her, but when he woke the next morning, it was to find that the princess had disappeared. And worse, that she had prized off the stone he wore instead of a heart and had taken it with her."

"Not a princess," Julienne whispered. "And you've never been a fool."

"Six months passed," he said, a faintly reproving note in his voice. "And the fool knew that he was not the same. His stone was gone, and that meant that he could feel that beating, untamable organ beneath. Suddenly, there was blood in his veins. Suddenly, he wanted things he knew he couldn't have. But he ignored it all, and assumed that if he locked himself away in eternal winter, he could find another stone. The world has no shortage of stones, after all."

Julienne's hand was still there on his chest, splayed wide over his flat pectoral muscle, and all she felt was his heart. The kick of it, insistent and strong.

No stones to be found.

"One day, the princess returned. She gazed at our fool, and to his astonishment, he could see in her eyes that what she saw was a hero. 'Look,' she said, and showed him her big, round belly, swollen with child. 'I have taken the stone that lay upon your heart, and see what I've made with it.'"

"A son," Julienne whispered.

"A son," he agreed. "But the fool knew that he was no hero, you see. And more, he was afraid of the princess, and the things she made him feel, and that hollow where his stone once lay. He knew that the princess was filled with light, and it was only a matter of time before she looked deep enough to see that there was nothing in him but darkness. He had an idea. He would marry the princess, and pile stones on top of her, muting her light. Saving himself in the process."

"Some princesses like stones," Julienne argued, astonished to hear the thickness in her voice. "Or they wouldn't take them from unsuspecting hearts in the first place, would they?"

"A princess might like to collect stones," Cristiano said, shaking his head at her. "But no one likes to have them stacked on top of their chest. Crushing out the will to live. The fool kept going, for he knew no other way. Every day he lay another stone upon the princess, and every day, he watched the light in her fade. Until one day, he realized that when she looked at him, all she saw was stone. That he was no longer a hero at all. And the fool knew then that if he continued along this path, it would only end one way. First he would kill the princess, as surely as if he choked her with his own hand. And then, inevitably, he would do the same to his son."

"Cristiano," she said.

And it was only his name. But it held whole worlds in it.

"More than that, he understood at last that the ogre and the troll were neither kings nor jailers, but had once been fools themselves. And once he understood that, everywhere he looked, he saw the stones his ancestors had piled up like walls."

She tried again, but she couldn't seem to speak. And she knew she didn't have stones on her chest, but love. So much love it hurt.

"That was when the fool remembered there had been another princess, long ago. A princess so feared that every ogre and troll in the kingdom called her a witch instead. And the fool ran, then, over the hills and into the forest. And he found an old woman who had once been a princess living alone in a cottage on the edge of a deep, dark wood."

"Your grandmother."

"A fool is a fool until the very end," Cristiano said. "'How can I help the princess?' he asked the old woman. 'How can I dislodge the stones enough to keep her breathing?' The old woman laughed, and she told him that the stone was a stone. It could never be changed. It was weight and heft, and when piled upon a princess would crush her, sure enough. "But the princess took a stone and made a son of it,' the fool argued."

Julienne's heart beat so hard, she wondered if she was made of stone herself.

"The old woman looked him straight in the eye. And she said, 'She didn't take a stone from you, child. She took your heart. And all you've done since is pretend you can function without it.'"

Cristiano smiled then, and Julienne held her breath.

"'You can, but you must kill her first in order to do it. And when you're done killing her, you must destroy your son, so he too becomes a fool. A fool becomes an ogre or troll, and if you squint, you can see which one he'll be. Which one you are.'"

"She sounds like a wise woman," Julienne managed to say, feeling wrecked. And a bit dizzy, too. "And scary, if I'm honest." She shifted where she sat, searching his face. "And I love a fairy tale, Cristiano, but I really would love to jump to the end of this one. The 'they lived happily ever after' part. Is that where we're headed?"

Though she wasn't sure what she'd do if he said no.

He held her gaze. Then he reached into the pocket of his trousers and pulled something out. And she didn't know why she was holding her breath again, because she already wore his rings. Beautiful, priceless works of stone and metal that declared her not only his, but forever a Cassara bride. His wife, no matter what.

Still, she watched as he opened his palm.

And then she blinked.

Because sitting there in his hand was a stone. At first she thought it was misshapen—but then she realized.

It looked like a heart.

"I'm not sure I have ever loved anything in my life," Cristiano told her, his voice deep and strong. "I have long hated the word. I have considered it nothing but the harbinger of doom, if I am honest. But I can think of no other word that explains how I feel about you, Julienne. You are the sun, the stars, the moon. You are all the light in the world, and I do not deserve you, and I don't know that I ever will. You think I saved you, when all the while, you must know that you are the one who has saved me. You took the stone away from my heart and taught me how to make it beat again. You have loved me completely, always. You are carrying my son. Everything is dark and cold without you. Me most of all."

She whispered his name again, but this time, perhaps it was a kind of incantation.

Hope, love and joy.

Cristiano.

"You already have my heart," he said. "I want you to have this, too. Because if I keep it, I think we both know that I will use whatever stones I have to build as many walls as possible. But not you, my beautiful Julienne. You make life. You make love. And I want nothing else than to dedicate myself to making you happy."

"Cristiano," she said, and this time, he did not cut her off. And she did not falter. "I love you. And I don't want to be a princess. You are not a fool, and I am your wife, and we will love each other as best we can, for as long as we can, so that our son grows up and doesn't spend his time worried about stones and ogres and trolls. But rather, happiness. Family. Love. All the things that make life worth living."

"I can think of no better happy-ever-after than that," he said, there against her mouth.

This time, when he kissed her, it tasted like forever.

And kiss by kiss, and stone by stone, they made it so.

CHAPTER THIRTEEN

JULIENNE WENT INTO labor the following morning, and by nightfall, their son was born.

And in Cristiano's wholly unbiased opinion, he was perfect.

They named him Pietro, which meant rock, because he was the greatest magic either one of them could imagine. And something far bigger and better than a mere stone.

And the more Cristiano allowed himself to love, the more magic there was to be found.

It took him the better part of a year, but he convinced Paola to start attending family functions, such as they were. To meet her great-grandson, and better still, the woman who had convinced a Cassara man to change.

"Perhaps it is not me who is the witch, then," the old woman cackled with glee, the first time she and Julienne met.

"I will take that as the highest compliment imaginable," Julienne replied.

It took him another year to convince Paola to move into the villa, where she could be mistress of the house at last. And his grandmother might have been in her nineties, but she ran the villa with an iron fist. And ordered Cristiano, Pietro and the three other sons Julienne bore him around at her leisure.

"It is not difficult to make a good man," the old woman told him on her hundredth birthday, grinning at him over her cane. "All it takes is a woman's firm hand."

Cristiano could not disagree.

But the hands he preferred on him belonged to his wife.

Julienne was his north star, his lodestone. She carried his babies, she raised his sons and when she was not busy creating tiny humans, she served on the Cassara Corporation board as well.

And, finally, together, they made it the family company it never had been in his grandfather's hands.

"That's because you are the man your grandfather never was," Julienne told him, year after year. "You love your wife. You would die for your family. You have honored your grandmother, and yes, Cristiano, you have rescued each and every one of us. Over and over again."

But Cristiano always knew the truth.

Julienne might have been the one to walk into that bar, determined to sell herself. But she had been the one to do the rescuing.

"I love you," he told her, every day of their lives.

And better still, showed her.

In any way he could, in every way that mattered, he showed her.

How he loved her. How crucial she was not only to his happiness, but to the mechanics that kept the world turning. How perfect she was and always had been, just as she was.

And in tougher times, or when things seemed the darkest, they would take out that stone that was shaped like a heart, and it would make them laugh.

Cristiano would tell her stories about ogres and trolls and terrible fools. Julienne would tell him stories about princesses who were born on hilltops, who came down to the sea to find their Prince Charmings.

Again and again, they wove their stories around themselves until they were right again.

Until they were whole.

"Happy-ever-after isn't made," Julienne liked to say as they lay in their bed, still wrapped around each other tightly twenty years on. "It's mended. The days are the thread, the years are the colors, and all we have to do is sew."

"I love you," Cristiano told her. *"Ti amo, mi amore. Tu mi completi."*

His heart, his love, his wife.

His whole life, gleaming there before him. Light and joy.

And then he rolled her over, and showed her how he loved her in the language he was most fluent in, once again.

Until she sang their love back to him, the way he loved best.

The way she always did, and always would, all the rest of their days.

* * * * *

Lost in the magic of
The Italian's Pregnant Cinderella*?*
Discover more stories by Caitlin Crews!

Untamed Billionaire's Innocent Bride
His Two Royal Secrets
Unwrapping the Innocent's Secret
Secrets of His Forbidden Cinderella

Available now

WE HOPE YOU ENJOYED
THIS BOOK FROM

◆ HARLEQUIN

PRESENTS

Escape to exotic locations where passion knows no bounds.

Welcome to the glamorous lives of royals and billionaires, where passion knows no bounds. Be swept into a world of luxury, wealth and exotic locations.

8 NEW BOOKS AVAILABLE EVERY MONTH!

#3809 CLAIMING THE VIRGIN'S BABY
by Jennie Lucas

Surrogate Rosalie realizes she can't bear to give away the child she's carrying for a childless Italian couple. She flies to Venice to beg forgiveness, only to discover billionaire Alex is a widower... and he had no idea she was expecting his baby!

#3810 THE SECRET KEPT FROM THE KING
by Clare Connelly

Sheikh Sariq is intrigued when Daisy declines his summons to his palace. Yet finding out she's secretly pregnant demands dramatic action! She's far from a suitable bride...but for their baby, he'll crown her. If Daisy will accept!

#3811 HIS SECRETARY'S NINE-MONTH NOTICE
by Cathy Williams

Handing in her notice was not part of dedicated Violet's plan...and definitely not because she's carrying her boss's baby! Still, nothing is quite as unexpected as Matt's reaction. He wants his child—and Violet!

#3812 THE GREEK'S UNKNOWN BRIDE
by Abby Green

Sasha's life changes beyond recognition after a shocking accident—her amnesia has made sure of that. She can't even remember marrying Apollo, her devastatingly handsome Greek husband! Although she does remember their intimate, searing passion...

#3813 A HIDDEN HEIR TO REDEEM HIM
Feuding Billionaire Brothers
by Dani Collins

Kiara could never regret the consequence of her one delicious night with Val—despite his coldheartedness. Yet behind Val's reputation is another man—revealed only in their passionate moments alone. Could she give *that* man a second chance?

#3814 CROWNING HIS UNLIKELY PRINCESS
by Michelle Conder

Cassidy's boss, Logan, is about to become king! She's busy trying to organize his royal diary—*and* handle the desire he's suddenly awakened! But when Logan reveals he craves her, too, Cassidy must decide: Could she *really* be his princess?

#3815 CONTRACTED TO HER GREEK ENEMY
by Annie West

Stephanie would love to throw tycoon Damen's outrageous proposal back in his face, but the truth is she must save her penniless family. Their contract says they can't kiss again...but Steph might soon regret that clause!

#3816 THE SPANIARD'S WEDDING REVENGE
by Jackie Ashenden

Securing Leonie's hand in marriage would allow Cristiano to take the one thing his enemy cares about. His first step? Convincing his newest—most *defiant*—employee to meet him at the altar!

---

*Sheikh Sariq is intrigued when Daisy declines his
summons to his palace. Yet finding out she's secretly
pregnant demands dramatic action! She's far from a
suitable bride...but for their baby he'll crown her.
If Daisy will accept...*

*Read on for a sneak preview of
Clare Connelly's next story for Harlequin Presents,*
The Secret Kept from the King.

"No." He held on to her wrist as though he could tell she was
about to run from the room. "Stop."

Her eyes lifted to his and she jerked on her wrist so she could
lift her fingers to her eyes and brush away her tears. Panic was
filling her, panic and disbelief at the mess she found herself in.

"How is this upsetting to you?" he asked more gently,
pressing his hands to her shoulders, stroking his thumbs over her
collarbone. "We agreed at the hotel that we could only have two
nights together, and you were fine with that. I'm offering you three
months on exactly those same terms, and you're acting as though
I've asked you to parade naked through the streets of Shajarah."

"You're ashamed of me," she said simply. "In New York we
were two people who wanted to be together. What you're proposing
turns me into your possession."

He stared at her, his eyes narrowed. "The money I will give you
is beside the point."

More tears sparkled on her lashes. "Not to me it's not."

"Then don't take the money," he said urgently. "Come to the
RKH and be my lover because you want to be with me."

"I can't." Tears fell freely down her face now. "I need that
money. I need it."

A muscle jerked in his jaw. "So have both."

"No, you don't understand."

She was a live wire of panic but she had to tell him, so that he understood why his offer was so revolting to her. She pulled away from him, pacing toward the windows, looking out on this city she loved. The trees at Bryant Park whistled in the fall breeze and she watched them for a moment, remembering the first time she'd seen them. She'd been a little girl, five, maybe six, and her dad had been performing at the restaurant on the fringes of the park. She'd worn her very best dress and, despite the heat, tights that were so uncomfortable she could vividly remember that feeling now. But the park had been beautiful and her dad's music had, as always, filled her heart with pleasure and joy.

Sariq was behind her now; she felt him, but didn't turn to look at him.

"I'm glad you were so honest with me today. It makes it easier for me, in a way, because I know exactly how you feel, how you see me and what you want from me." Her voice was hollow, completely devoid of emotion when she had a thousand feelings throbbing inside her.

He said nothing. He didn't try to deny it. Good. Just as she'd said, it was easier when things were black-and-white.

"I don't want money so I can attend Juilliard, Your Highness." It pleased her to use his title, to use that as a point of difference, to put a line between them that neither of them could cross.

Silence. Heavy, loaded with questions. And finally, "Then what do you need such a sum for?"

She bit down on her lip, her tummy squeezing tight. "I'm pregnant. And you're the father."

Don't miss
The Secret Kept from the King,
available May 2020 wherever
Harlequin Presents books and ebooks are sold.

Harlequin.com

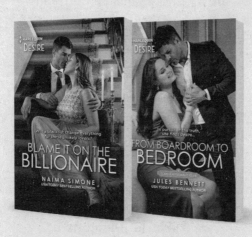

Love Harlequin romance?

DISCOVER.

Be the first to find out about promotions, news and exclusive content!

Facebook.com/HarlequinBooks

Twitter.com/HarlequinBooks

Instagram.com/HarlequinBooks

Pinterest.com/HarlequinBooks

ReaderService.com

EXPLORE.

Sign up for the Harlequin e-newsletter and download a free book from any series at **TryHarlequin.com**

CONNECT.

Join our Harlequin community to share your thoughts and connect with other romance readers!
Facebook.com/groups/HarlequinConnection